Short Stories for Seniors:

5-Minute Read-Alouds in Large Print with Memory Prompts and Conversation Starters

Ted Fraley

Disclaimer

The information provided in this book is for educational and entertainment purposes only. While every effort has been made to ensure accuracy and completeness, the author and publisher assume no responsibility for errors, omissions, or contrary interpretation of the subject matter herein. This book is not intended to provide legal, financial, medical, or professional advice. The reader accepts responsibility for their own decisions and actions.

Table of Contents

About me and Why I Wrote This Book

Hello! Let me share a little about myself and what inspired me to create this collection of stories.

Throughout my life, I've always felt that each of us holds a treasure chest of memories and experiences worth sharing. Our stories connect us to one another, offering warmth, laughter, and sometimes even gentle lessons. I've always believed deeply in the power of storytelling, not only as a way to entertain but also as a beautiful tool for bringing people closer.

This book was born from that belief. It began as a reflection on some of my most treasured memories, like building a kite from scratch, spending warm afternoons in my grandmother's kitchen, or the simple joy of being with friends and family. Soon enough, these personal recollections blossomed into something more universal, stories that could resonate with anyone who cherishes life's everyday moments.

I chose to dedicate this collection to seniors because memories often take on a special meaning later in life. They comfort us, offer perspective, and remind us of the rich experiences that have made us who we are. My greatest wish is that these stories become companions that spark your own cherished recollections and encourage meaningful conversations with the people you care about.

I wrote this book out of genuine admiration and respect for the journey you've traveled. May these stories bring you smiles, warmth, and perhaps inspire you to share some of your own wonderful memories along the way.

Warmly,

Ted

Chapter 1: Childhood Memories

Childhood holds countless simple experiences that remain vivid even decades later. It could be the smell of your grandmother's homemade cookies filling the kitchen, the gentle whisper of a kite sailing through a clear sky, or the excited shouts from neighborhood children during an unexpected snow day. Perhaps you remember the freedom of pedaling your bike alone for the first time, the warmth of friendship as you shared secrets on the playground, or the quiet thrill of discovering the shelves in your local library. These stories are here to bring you back to those carefree days and remind you of feelings that have never fully faded. As you read, allow yourself the pleasure of reliving those small adventures and joyful mishaps. Feel free to pause and think about your own experiences—your favorite birthday party, the comforting routine of bedtime stories, or the simple happiness of chasing fireflies at dusk. Childhood memories carry an ease and innocence that offer comfort throughout life. In reading these short stories, you'll likely discover a pleasant familiarity, maybe even a forgotten moment resurfacing like an old friend. Let's revisit that special time together, when joy was abundant, life was uncomplicated, and every day held a fresh reason to smile.

The Day of the Red Kite

Jacob sat cross-legged on his front porch, surrounded by bits of string, sticks he'd gathered beneath the backyard oak, and sheets of vivid red tissue paper. It was the first warm day of spring—perfect weather, he decided, to finally build his first kite.

He carefully tied two thin sticks into a cross shape, wrapping them tight with twine from his mother's kitchen drawer. Next, he gently spread the tissue paper, feeling it crinkle softly beneath his fingers. After a few minutes of careful work, his kite began to take shape—simple, but promising.

When he was done, Jacob held the kite up to the sunlight. It glowed warmly, casting a faint red reflection on the porch. His mother peeked out the door, smiling. "That looks wonderful, Jacob. Do you think it'll fly?"

Jacob's eyes sparkled with determination. "It will," he answered, hoping he was right.

He grabbed his kite, tucked a roll of twine into his pocket, and raced toward the open field behind their home. The spring grass tickled his bare feet, soft and cool beneath his steps. The field stretched ahead, wide and empty, with a breeze whispering gently through the tall grass—perfect for flying.

Jacob raised the kite above his head, feeling his heart beat faster. Holding tightly to the string, he started to run. The wind brushed past his face and caught beneath the kite, tugging lightly at his fingertips. He ran faster, feeling the air lift his creation higher with each step.

At first, the kite wobbled nervously. Jacob held his breath. "Please," he whispered, "just fly." Then, suddenly, a stronger gust swept underneath, carrying it skyward with confidence.

Jacob's heart leaped as he watched the kite soar upward, the red shape bright and vibrant against the clear, blue sky. It moved smoothly now, climbing higher and higher, tugging gently on the string in his hand.

Laughing, he sprinted across the field, his kite dancing above him. The air filled with soft rustling sounds—the quiet whisper of paper, the faint hum of twine vibrating gently between his fingers. Jacob imagined what the kite might see from up there—his small house, the oak tree, and fields stretching far away.

He glanced back toward home, waving excitedly to his mother, who had come outside to watch, shielding her eyes from the sunlight. She waved back, smiling brightly.

After what felt like hours of joy, Jacob carefully guided the kite downward, pulling it in little by little until it drifted softly into his hands. Breathless, he admired his creation—still perfect, still beautiful.

He walked slowly back home, the kite tucked safely under his arm. Proud happiness filled him; he'd built something simple and made it fly. It felt like a small, sweet victory he would remember forever.

That night, Jacob placed the kite gently on his dresser, where the moonlight made its red paper glow softly. Already, he couldn't wait to fly it again.

Memory Prompts:

- Did you ever make your own toy or game?
- Can you recall the first time you felt proud of something you built?
- What outdoor activities did you enjoy most as a child?

Conversation Starters:

- Would you rather fly a kite at the park or at the beach?
- If you could pick a color for your dream kite, which would it be?
- Do you enjoy watching others fly kites today?

Grandma's Kitchen Secrets

Sarah loved the days spent in Grandma's kitchen. Every Saturday, she'd hurry down the familiar stone path that led to the cozy house at the end of the street, where warm scents greeted her even before she reached the door.

Stepping inside, Sarah would close her eyes, breathing deeply. The comforting aroma of cinnamon, apples, and buttery pastry floated from the oven, wrapping around her like a soft blanket. Grandma stood at the kitchen counter, sleeves rolled up and apron dusted with flour, smiling warmly.

"Ready to help, Sarah?" Grandma asked.

Sarah nodded eagerly, washing her small hands at the sink. Her feet balanced on the step stool, bringing her just high enough to see over the counter. Today was apple pie day—Sarah's favorite. Grandma placed a bowl of freshly peeled apples in front of her. Carefully, Sarah sprinkled sugar and cinnamon over the slices, stirring gently. The mixture sparkled, making her mouth water.

"What makes your pies taste so good, Grandma?" Sarah asked curiously. Grandma winked, a twinkle in her eyes.

"It's a special secret ingredient," she whispered. "Maybe you'll guess it today."

Sarah tilted her head thoughtfully but kept stirring. The kitchen filled with the gentle bubbling of simmering apples, mixed with Grandma's soft humming of old songs Sarah loved but didn't know the words to.

Grandma rolled out dough, working quickly and gracefully. Sarah tried to copy her movements, pressing tiny fingerprints into the floury dough. Her hands weren't quite as skilled yet, but Grandma always said mistakes were part of the magic. Together they carefully arranged the apples inside the crust, covering them neatly with another thin blanket of pastry. Sarah pressed the edges gently with a fork, smiling at the pattern she made.

As Grandma slid the pie into the oven, Sarah's eyes followed, eagerly anticipating the sweet result.

While they waited, Grandma poured two glasses of cold milk, and they sat at the old wooden table, sunlight warming their shoulders. Sarah swung her legs beneath the chair, sipping milk and sharing stories about school and friends. Grandma listened carefully, nodding and laughing at all the right places. Soon, the timer rang, and Grandma carefully pulled out the golden-brown pie. It looked perfect, the crust lightly sprinkled with sugar, steam gently rising, filling the kitchen with sweetness.

Sarah took the first bite, savoring the warm apples and buttery crust melting in her mouth. Her eyes widened with joy.

"I think I figured it out!" she announced triumphantly.

"Oh? What's my secret?" Grandma asked, leaning forward.

Sarah smiled shyly, then whispered, "It's love."

Grandma hugged her tightly, kissing her forehead. "Exactly right," she said softly. "Love makes everything taste better."

They finished their pie, talking and laughing until the afternoon sun dipped low. Walking home, Sarah felt warm and content. She knew now why nothing tasted quite like Grandma's pies. It was a secret she planned to remember forever.

Memory Prompts:

- What dish reminds you of home?
- Did someone in your family love to cook or bake?
- Do you remember helping in the kitchen as a child?

Conversation Starters:

- Do you prefer baking or cooking savory meals?
- What's your favorite dessert now?
- If you could invite anyone to share a meal, who would it be?

The Summer Bicycle

Tommy stood nervously beside his shiny blue bicycle. His dad had just removed the training wheels, and suddenly the bike felt big and unfamiliar.

"You can do this," Dad encouraged, giving Tommy's shoulder a reassuring squeeze.

Tommy wasn't sure. Without the training wheels, his bike looked unsteady. But he'd watched his older sister ride freely down the street all summer, laughing with friends. He wanted that same freedom.

Dad held the bike steady while Tommy climbed on. His feet barely reached the ground, but he gripped the handlebars firmly, determined to try.

"Ready?" Dad asked.

Tommy took a deep breath and nodded. "Ready."

Dad gently pushed the bike forward, jogging alongside. Tommy pedaled cautiously, wobbling slightly. His heart pounded. Just as he started to balance, the bike tilted sideways, and he tumbled onto the soft grass.

"You okay?" Dad asked, offering a hand.

Tommy brushed grass from his knees, feeling embarrassed but determined. "Let me try again."

They repeated this several times—each attempt lasting a bit longer, each fall softer. Tommy's confidence slowly grew. He pedaled faster, feeling steadier with every push forward.

"You're doing it, Tommy!" Dad shouted, smiling broadly. "Keep pedaling!"

Tommy realized suddenly he was riding alone. Dad had let go, and now Tommy soared forward, steady and smooth. A surge of excitement rushed through him. Wind whistled in his ears, the pedals spun effortlessly, and he laughed out loud with joy.

“Dad, look—I’m riding!” Tommy called over his shoulder.

“You sure are!” Dad cheered from behind. “Now turn around and ride back!”

A bit nervous but excited, Tommy gently turned the handlebars, making a wide circle back toward his dad. His balance held perfectly.

Tommy rode confidently back and forth, each pass stronger than before. His worries disappeared, replaced by pride and a thrilling sense of freedom. He imagined himself racing down neighborhood streets alongside his sister, joining friends on summer adventures.

Eventually, Tommy slowed down, carefully stopping beside his dad. He hopped off his bike, breathing heavily, cheeks flushed with pride.

“You did it, buddy,” Dad said warmly. “I knew you could.”

Tommy grinned. The scrapes on his knees didn’t matter. Today, he'd conquered something important, something he'd feared but had tried anyway.

That evening, as Tommy put his bike away, he felt taller somehow, more grown-up. Tomorrow, he’d ride further, faster. Maybe he’d race his sister down to the corner store. The possibilities felt endless.

As Tommy drifted off to sleep, his legs still tingled with excitement, and he knew one thing for certain—he couldn’t wait to ride again.

Memory Prompts:

- Who first taught you how to ride a bike?
- Do you remember your favorite bicycle?
- Where did you like to ride when you were young?

Conversation Starters:

- Would you rather ride through a quiet park or a busy town?
- What’s your favorite way to enjoy the outdoors now?
- Do you still enjoy cycling or walking more?

Schoolyard Secrets

Behind the old schoolhouse, near the chain-link fence covered in ivy, Ben and Danny crouched down low, giggling softly.

"This is our secret spot," Danny whispered, eyes sparkling with excitement.

Ben nodded, glancing around carefully. "Nobody else can know."

Every recess, they met here, away from the noisy playground and the crowded swings. Hidden behind the ivy, they felt like explorers discovering their own private world. Today, Ben had something special to show his best friend.

He reached into his jacket pocket, pulling out a small, shiny stone. It glittered brightly in the sunlight filtering through the leaves.

“Whoa,” Danny whispered, eyes wide. “Where’d you get it?”

“Found it near the creek,” Ben said proudly. “It’s probably treasure.”

They both stared at it quietly, imagining all the adventures this small, sparkling rock had been through. Danny reached into his own pocket and pulled out a smooth piece of blue sea glass.

“I found this at the beach,” Danny said. “Maybe it’s treasure too.”

The boys exchanged a serious look, then nodded. Carefully, they placed both items under a loose brick near the fence. It was their secret collection, hidden from everyone else.

“No one else can know,” Ben repeated firmly.

Danny smiled. “Best friends forever?”

“Forever,” Ben promised, bumping fists.

Suddenly, the school bell rang loudly, breaking the spell of their secret hideaway. Laughing, the boys scrambled up, brushing dirt from their knees as they ran back to class.

As the weeks passed, their secret collection grew. They added colorful feathers, old coins, and tiny shells, each item carefully chosen and hidden away. Behind the ivy fence, their friendship grew too—quietly and surely, strengthened by secrets and laughter.

Then one day, Danny came to recess looking sad.

“I’m moving away soon,” he said quietly, eyes fixed on his sneakers.

Ben felt a sudden lump in his throat. “But what about our secret spot?”

Danny smiled gently. “It’ll still be ours. Even if I’m not here.”

They sat quietly together that day, the noise of the playground fading into the background. Finally, Danny reached for the hidden brick, pulling out their treasures one last time.

“You keep these safe,” Danny said, handing the shiny stone back to Ben. “I’ll always remember our spot.”

Ben nodded, feeling comforted. “Me too. And if you ever come back, they’ll be right here.”

Danny smiled, hopeful again. “Promise?”

“Promise.”

When the bell rang, the boys stood slowly. Before heading back, they glanced once more at the ivy fence, their friendship safe and strong, just like the treasures they’d hidden.

Even years later, Ben never forgot their secret place behind the schoolyard fence, where friendship had taken root and grown quietly beneath the ivy.

Memory Prompts:

- Who was your closest friend in school?
- Did you ever share a secret place to meet?
- Can you recall a game you loved at recess?

Conversation Starters:

- Do you think childhood friendships last a lifetime?
- What’s a fun memory from your school days?
- Would you rather play indoors or outdoors as a child?

Snow Day Adventures

Anna woke early, her bedroom glowing brighter than usual. Curious, she leaped from bed, hurried to the window, and pressed her nose against the chilly glass. Outside, a fresh blanket of snow sparkled brightly beneath the morning sun.

"It snowed!" Anna shouted, racing downstairs to the kitchen.

Her mother was already up, stirring cocoa on the stove. She smiled warmly. "School is canceled today."

Anna jumped up and down excitedly, taking quick sips of cocoa before scrambling to put on layers of warm clothes—her heavy coat, wool hat, scarf, mittens, and thick boots. She could barely move, bundled up like a small penguin, but she didn't mind.

Outside, the air was crisp and cold, filling her lungs with freshness. Friends from the neighborhood were already gathered near the small hill behind her house, pulling sleds and laughing joyfully. Anna grabbed her wooden sled from the porch, waved goodbye to her mother, and trudged eagerly through the fluffy snow.

"Come on, Anna!" Michael called, waving her over. His cheeks were bright red from the cold, eyes sparkling with excitement. "Let's race!"

Together, they lined up at the top of the hill, positioning their sleds carefully. Anna's heart beat fast as she pushed off with her feet, gliding quickly down the snowy slope. Wind rushed past her face, and she laughed with delight, speeding toward the bottom.

When her sled finally came to a stop, she rolled onto the soft snow, laughing breathlessly. Michael landed beside her, grinning from ear to ear.

"Let's build the biggest snowman ever!" Anna suggested eagerly.

The children quickly got to work, rolling snowballs until they grew heavy and huge. Carefully stacking them, they shaped a friendly figure. Anna found two shiny black stones for eyes and Michael stuck a bright orange carrot right in the center as a nose. Anna wrapped her scarf gently around the snowman's neck, finishing him off perfectly.

“He’s wonderful,” she said proudly.

The friends played all day, tossing snowballs, making snow angels, and chasing each other through drifts that reached their knees. As the sun began to dip lower, turning the sky shades of pink and gold, Anna’s fingers felt numb, her nose tingling from the cold.

Waving goodbye to her friends, she stepped inside, warmth greeting her immediately. Removing her wet clothes and boots, she settled next to the fireplace. Her mother handed her another mug of cocoa, this one piled high with marshmallows, melting slowly into sweet, creamy foam.

“Did you have fun?” her mother asked softly, sitting beside her.

Anna nodded, sipping carefully. “It was the best day ever.”

Later, snug beneath her blankets, Anna listened to the gentle whisper of falling snow outside her window, creating a fresh white world once again. Sleepily, she hoped tomorrow would bring even more snowy adventures.

Memory Prompts:

- Did you ever have school canceled for snow?
- What winter activities did you enjoy most?
- Do you remember the clothes you wore in the snow?

Conversation Starters:

- Do you prefer snowy winters or warm summers?
- What’s your favorite winter drink?
- If you could visit anywhere in winter, where would you go?

The Little Radio Show

Every evening after supper, Sam's family gathered in the cozy living room around their old wooden radio. The polished wood gleamed softly in the lamplight, and its dials glowed amber as gentle static filled the room, signaling the start of their favorite show.

Sam settled onto the worn carpet, leaning comfortably against his father's chair. His mother sat on the sofa, knitting quietly, while his sister Molly curled up beside her with a small blanket. The family's dog, Max, stretched out nearby, content to snooze while voices floated through the room.

"Quiet now," his father whispered, gently turning up the volume. The static faded away, replaced by warm voices drifting out of the speaker, welcoming listeners to the evening program.

Sam loved listening to stories told by actors whose faces he never saw but whose voices he knew by heart. Tonight's tale was about brave adventurers exploring far-off jungles. As he listened, he imagined tall trees, thick vines, and hidden treasures. His eyes widened, and his heart raced with excitement at every twist and turn.

Occasionally, his mother chuckled softly, shaking her head at the heroes' silly mistakes. Molly hugged her blanket tighter whenever danger seemed close. Sam felt safe and happy, knowing that no matter what troubles the characters faced, the heroes always won in the end.

When the story ended, soft music filled the room. His parents quietly hummed along to the gentle tunes that reminded Sam of sleepy summer evenings. Sometimes, his mother and father shared quiet smiles across the room, their faces glowing in the warm lamplight.

One evening, after the music stopped, Sam glanced curiously at his father. "Did you listen to the radio when you were little?"

His father nodded, eyes thoughtful. "Every night. Just like this."

"Did you have the same shows?" Molly asked sleepily.

"Some of them," their father said warmly. "But my favorite was always the music. Your grandmother would dance sometimes, right here in this room."

Sam smiled, imagining his grandmother younger, dancing gracefully to the songs he now heard each night.

"Maybe we can dance too," Sam suggested softly.

His mother looked up, smiling brightly. Without another word, his father stood and gently took her hand. Together they moved slowly around the small room, gently swaying to the fading melody from the radio. Sam and Molly giggled quietly, watching their parents spin lightly over the carpet.

Even Max lifted his head, curious about the unusual movement. The family's laughter and the gentle music mixed together, filling the cozy living room with warmth and happiness.

Eventually, the radio went silent, and everyone yawned, ready for bed. Sam hugged his parents goodnight, feeling safe and warm inside. He knew that tomorrow evening they'd gather again around the old radio, ready for new stories, soft music, and perhaps even another dance.

As he drifted off to sleep, he smiled, comforted by the thought of another perfect evening waiting just around the corner.

Memory Prompts:

- What radio shows or songs do you remember from childhood?
- Did your family gather around a radio or TV together?
- Can you recall a tune that always makes you smile?

Conversation Starters:

- Do you prefer listening to music or watching movies?
- Which voice from your past do you wish you could hear again?
- Do you enjoy listening to the radio today?

The First Library Card

Alex couldn't believe the day had finally arrived. He stood nervously in front of the old stone library, gripping his mother's hand, eyes wide with excitement. Today, he was getting his very first library card.

Inside, the library was quiet and welcoming, filled with tall shelves of colorful books. Alex breathed in deeply, loving the comforting scent of paper and ink.

At the front desk, Mrs. Reed, the kind librarian, smiled warmly. "Hello, Alex. I hear today's special?"

Alex nodded shyly. "I'm getting my library card."

Mrs. Reed handed him a small card printed neatly with his name. "Here you go. Now you can choose books to take home."

Alex's heart swelled with pride as he carefully placed the card in his pocket, feeling important. Holding his mother's hand, he wandered down the rows of bookshelves, looking up in wonder at all the stories waiting for him.

"Which book should I pick first?" he asked softly.

His mother smiled gently. "Any one you want."

Excitedly, Alex ran his fingers along the spines of countless books, stopping when he saw a familiar title. He pulled it from the shelf, eyes wide. It had colorful illustrations of dragons and knights. His favorite.

"This one," he said happily.

They continued walking, Alex quickly gathering a small stack of books, each more exciting than the last. When he carried them back to Mrs. Reed's desk, she stamped each one carefully.

"These are due back in two weeks," she said kindly. "Happy reading!"

At home, Alex immediately settled onto the couch, books piled beside him. He opened the dragon story first, diving eagerly into a world of adventure. With each page, he traveled to magical lands, battled fierce dragons, and befriended brave knights.

Days passed, and Alex read constantly—after breakfast, before bed, even curled up beneath blankets by flashlight. He discovered stories of brave explorers, distant planets, and hidden treasures. His imagination soared.

Two weeks flew by quickly, and Alex returned to the library, eager for more adventures. Mrs. Reed greeted him warmly, pleased to see his excitement.

"Did you enjoy your books?" she asked.

Alex nodded vigorously. "I loved them. Can I pick more today?"

She smiled. "Of course. Your library card lets you explore as many stories as you wish."

Alex wandered through the shelves, choosing new books and discovering worlds he'd never imagined. Each visit filled him with wonder, knowing endless possibilities awaited him.

Years later, Alex would always recall the day he received his first library card—the small piece of paper that opened doors to infinite adventures, helping him dream, explore, and grow.

Memory Prompts:

- What was the first book you ever loved?
- Did you have a library or bookshop you visited often?
- Can you remember a teacher who encouraged you to read?

Conversation Starters:

- Do you prefer novels, short stories, or poetry?
- Which book would you recommend to someone younger?
- Do you enjoy libraries or bookstores more?

Fireflies in the Yard

The backyard buzzed softly on warm summer evenings. Crickets hummed quietly from the grass, blending into the gentle whispers of leaves swaying in the breeze. Tonight, though, something special was happening. Emma and her cousins were chasing fireflies.

As the sun dipped low, twilight turned the sky into soft shades of blue and purple. One by one, tiny lights began to flicker and glow. Emma stood barefoot in the cool grass, her eyes wide with wonder as she watched the tiny flashes floating gently through the air.

"Let's catch them!" her cousin Lily called excitedly, holding a glass jar with small holes poked in the lid. Emma nodded eagerly, following Lily through the yard, their bare feet damp with dew.

Slowly and carefully, Emma stretched out her hands, waiting patiently. Suddenly, a small yellow glow hovered just in front of her. Holding her breath, she cupped her hands softly around it. She peeked between her fingers, smiling as the tiny firefly blinked gently, lighting her palm.

"I got one!" she shouted proudly, running to show Lily. They giggled, carefully placing the tiny glowing creature inside the jar.

As darkness deepened, the yard became a sea of twinkling lights. Emma and her cousins chased the gentle flashes, laughing as fireflies danced just out of reach. They ran in circles, their arms outstretched, faces bright with excitement.

"Why do they glow?" Emma asked softly, holding up the jar filled with gently blinking fireflies.

"Maybe it's magic," Lily whispered, her eyes shining.

They gathered near the porch, quietly sitting together in the soft grass, their jar glowing warmly between them. The yard had turned into something enchanting, the air filled with quiet wonder.

Emma's grandmother stepped onto the porch, smiling at their adventure. "Did you catch many?"

"Yes, lots!" Emma answered proudly.

Her grandmother bent down slowly, studying the little lights. "Fireflies bring special memories. They remind us how beautiful small moments can be."

Emma thought about that, watching the fireflies blink softly. Their gentle glow felt comforting, magical even.

After a while, Lily stood up and carefully opened the jar. One by one, the fireflies drifted slowly back into the night sky, floating gracefully, tiny lights returning to their gentle dance.

The cousins lay quietly on their backs, staring up at the stars that seemed to sparkle just as gently as the fireflies. Emma felt happy, surrounded by family, knowing tonight would always be a special memory—a warm summer evening full of gentle laughter and magical lights.

Long after summer ended, whenever Emma saw the soft flicker of a firefly, she would smile, remembering that night in the yard and the simple joy of catching tiny glowing wonders beneath a starry sky.

Memory Prompts:

- Did you ever catch fireflies or butterflies as a child?
- Do you recall summer nights outdoors?
- What childhood games did you play outside after dark?

Conversation Starters:

- Do you prefer warm summer nights or crisp autumn evenings?
- What outdoor activity brings you joy today?
- If you could relive one childhood summer, which would it be?

The First Time at the Movies

Billy stood outside the theater, holding his father's hand tightly. He stared up at the big, glowing sign that announced the afternoon feature in bright letters. This was Billy's first time at the movies, and his heart raced with excitement.

Stepping into the dim lobby, Billy inhaled deeply. The air smelled like fresh popcorn and sweet candy. His eyes widened at the colorful posters lining the walls, showing brave cowboys and funny cartoon animals. People bustled around, smiling and chatting quietly, their arms filled with treats and drinks.

"Would you like popcorn?" his father asked, gently squeezing Billy's hand.

"Yes, please!" Billy answered, bouncing slightly on his toes.

They walked up to the counter, and soon Billy held his own small box of warm, buttery popcorn. He tasted a few kernels, savoring the salty flavor that melted in his mouth.

When the theater doors opened, Billy stepped carefully inside. The room felt enormous, filled with rows and rows of soft seats facing a giant, blank screen. The lights were low, creating a cozy darkness. Billy and his father chose seats in the middle, and Billy settled back, popcorn in his lap, eyes fixed eagerly ahead.

Suddenly, the room darkened completely, and the screen came alive with brilliant colors. Billy jumped a little, surprised by how big and bright it was. Music played, and cartoons danced across the screen, making him giggle and lean forward in excitement.

Soon, the main feature began. It was a thrilling adventure about explorers discovering a hidden jungle. Billy felt like he was there, walking alongside brave heroes through thick forests, crossing rivers, and escaping wild animals. His heart beat quickly during the tense moments, and he laughed with joy during funny scenes.

Throughout the movie, Billy barely blinked, completely absorbed by the magical world unfolding before him. He even forgot about his popcorn, now cold in his lap, as he watched the heroes triumphantly complete their journey.

When the lights slowly brightened again, Billy blinked and looked around, amazed to find himself back in the theater. He turned to his father, smiling widely.

"That was incredible!" Billy whispered in awe.

His father chuckled, helping Billy gather his coat and leftover snacks. As they stepped out into the late afternoon sunlight, Billy felt like he'd just returned from an exciting journey himself.

Walking home, Billy couldn't stop talking about the characters, the adventure, and how big everything had seemed on the screen.

"Can we go again sometime?" he asked eagerly.

His father smiled warmly. "Of course. There are many more adventures waiting for us."

Billy nodded happily, already dreaming of their next movie trip. He knew he'd never forget today—the day he discovered the magic of the movies.

Memory Prompts:

- Do you remember your first movie theater visit?
- Who did you go with?
- Did you have a favorite actor or actress growing up?

Conversation Starters:

- Do you prefer comedies, musicals, or westerns?
- Do you enjoy watching movies at home or at the theater?
- What's a film you would love to watch again on a big screen?

Birthday Balloons and Surprises

It was early morning when Jamie opened his eyes. Sunshine streamed through the window, gently waking him. A smile spread across his face as he realized today was his birthday.

Excited voices echoed downstairs, and Jamie jumped from bed, hurrying down to the kitchen. Bright balloons floated gently against the ceiling, colorful and cheerful, swaying slightly each time the door opened.

“Happy Birthday!” his mother called warmly, wrapping him in a tight hug.

Jamie beamed, taking in the festive sight. The table held a homemade chocolate cake, frosted with thick icing and decorated with tiny candies, Jamie’s favorite. Next to it stood several small gifts, each wrapped carefully in bright paper.

After breakfast, Jamie’s friends arrived, spilling laughter and excitement into the backyard. They played simple games—tag, hide and seek, and relay races. Jamie ran until his cheeks flushed pink, his laughter mingling with the joyful shouts of his friends.

Then came the presents. Sitting beneath the big oak tree, Jamie opened them carefully, savoring each surprise. He unwrapped a new baseball, a coloring book, and a handmade picture frame decorated with seashells. Every gift made him smile wider, feeling warmth from each thoughtful gesture.

Finally, his grandmother handed him a small package, wrapped neatly in paper dotted with tiny balloons. “Open this one slowly,” she said gently.

Curious, Jamie peeled the paper away. Inside was a wooden box, polished smooth. He carefully opened the lid, discovering a shiny silver compass. He held it gently, admiring its detailed arrow and the delicate engraving of his initials.

“It belonged to your grandfather,” his grandmother explained softly. “He always found his way home with it, and now it’s yours.”

Jamie's heart swelled. He had never received something so special before. Carefully, he tucked the compass into his pocket, deciding it would always stay with him.

The afternoon continued with laughter and cake, Jamie blowing out candles and making a quiet wish. Later, as guests began leaving, he hugged each friend goodbye, his heart full.

That evening, Jamie sat quietly on the porch, the compass warm in his hand. Balloons still drifted gently inside, their bright colors softening in the fading sunlight. He watched the evening sky turn deep shades of purple and orange, grateful for the simple yet perfect birthday.

His mother came to sit beside him, wrapping an arm around his shoulders. "Did you have a good day?" she asked softly.

Jamie nodded, smiling gently. "The best ever."

As night settled in, Jamie climbed into bed, the compass placed carefully beside him. He drifted off feeling loved, secure, and deeply happy, knowing this birthday—filled with balloons, games, and surprises—would stay in his memory forever.

Memory Prompts:

- What birthday do you remember most clearly?
- Did you ever get a handmade gift?
- What games did you play at parties as a child?

Conversation Starters:

- Do you enjoy big parties or small gatherings?
- What's your favorite kind of birthday cake?
- If you could plan your perfect birthday, what would it look like?

Chapter 2: Family Gatherings

Family gatherings fill our lives with warmth, laughter, and the comfort of familiar voices. These special times bring relatives together around tables covered with favorite dishes, in living rooms filled with stories, and in backyards or parks where simple picnics become treasured events. Maybe you recall the inviting smell of Sunday dinner, or sitting shoulder-to-shoulder with cousins, eating sandwiches and lemonade beneath the shade of a big tree. Perhaps your family had a special tablecloth reserved only for holidays, carrying memories of countless celebrations. Even small moments, like posing for family photographs, exploring attics filled with forgotten treasures, or listening to grandparents share their wisdom on a garden bench, hold a quiet magic that lasts a lifetime. Each of the stories that follow is meant to spark memories of your own family traditions, large or small. As you read, you might recall noisy dinners filled with jokes and laughter, annual fairs where rides and treats delighted everyone, or quiet evenings when the family gathered around the radio. Whatever your memories may be, family gatherings are about connection and belonging. So, settle in comfortably and let these stories gently remind you of those people and places that have always felt like home.

The Sunday Roast

When I was young, Sunday mornings meant waking up to the smell of roasting meat drifting through the house. It was our weekly family ritual. My grandmother would be in the kitchen early, her apron dusted with flour, humming softly as she peeled potatoes and chopped carrots. I still remember the rhythm of her knife tapping against the cutting board, mixing with the soft bubbling from pots on the stove.

My mother set the dining table meticulously, unfolding the good tablecloth embroidered with tiny flowers, saved only for Sundays and holidays. We kids were always given small chores, like arranging napkins or filling water glasses. I always felt important placing forks and knives just right, trying to mirror my mother's careful precision.

By noon, the house would fill with laughter and conversation as relatives arrived one by one. My uncle Jim always brought a freshly baked loaf of bread from the bakery in town. Aunt Rose carried her famous apple pie, the crust perfectly browned, filling sweet and cinnamon-rich.

We would gather around the dining table, squeezing into chairs until elbows bumped gently against each other. As Grandma brought the roast from the oven, everyone paused, leaning forward slightly to admire the steaming golden centerpiece. My father would carefully carve the roast, handing slices to my mother to place onto each plate. I watched the juices pool beneath the meat, eager for that first taste.

Conversation flowed naturally, filling the room with stories about the week, jokes shared, and plans made for the days ahead. I remember how easily laughter came, bouncing from one end of the table to the other. Even disagreements felt gentler around that table, softened by good food and familiar comfort.

As we ate, I loved watching Grandma. Her eyes sparkled with satisfaction when someone praised her cooking, though she'd wave it off modestly. To her, it wasn't about compliments; it was about seeing the family gathered and happy.

After the meal, while the adults lingered over coffee, we kids would hurry outside. The yard was large enough for tag or hide-and-seek. Sometimes we sat on the porch steps, nibbling slices of Aunt Rose's pie, the flaky crust crumbling onto our fingers.

When it was time for everyone to leave, there were always long goodbyes. Grandma would hand out leftover packages wrapped neatly in foil, reminding each of us to visit soon. I recall the warmth of her hug, the comforting smell of the roast lingering on her clothes.

Even now, years later, Sunday dinners remain vivid in my memory. They taught me about family, about slowing down, and about enjoying simple moments. The meals were delicious, but what sticks with me most was the feeling of belonging. It wasn't fancy; it was simply ours.

Today, whenever I smell roast meat cooking or taste fresh apple pie, I return for a moment to those Sundays, to the laughter, and to Grandma, smiling proudly at a table full of loved ones.

Memory Prompts:

- Did your family have a traditional Sunday meal?
- Who usually cooked at home when you were young?
- Do you remember a favorite dish from family gatherings?

Conversation Starters:

- Do you prefer big meals or small, simple dinners?
- What dish would you choose for a family celebration?
- Who in your family was known as the best cook?

The Summer Picnic Under the Oak

On warm summer days, my family often had picnics under a large oak tree at the edge of the meadow near my grandparents' farm. My grandfather would spread an old checkered blanket on the grass, and everyone placed their baskets and bowls filled with food around its edges. We sat cross-legged, bumping knees and sharing plates, the shade from the oak's broad branches keeping us cool.

The basket my mother packed always contained thick ham sandwiches wrapped in wax paper, slices of sharp cheddar cheese, crisp dill pickles, and homemade potato salad. My aunt brought sweet corn muffins that she baked fresh each time. There was always lemonade, slightly tart and icy cold from the thermos. I remember hoping the basket also contained my favorite treat: soft chocolate chip cookies that my grandmother made just for me.

While the grown-ups relaxed, talking quietly or laughing loudly, we kids would eat quickly so we could play. My cousins and I would form teams and start a game of catch or kickball, the grass soft beneath our bare feet. Occasionally, a ball would bounce into the picnic area, causing the adults to playfully scold us with smiles on their faces.

Sometimes, instead of ball games, we'd gather around my older cousin, who knew card tricks and silly riddles. We'd lean in close, fascinated as he shuffled and dealt the cards, amazed every time he guessed the right card or performed a trick we couldn't figure out.

After eating, the adults would drift into conversations about work, family news, or memories of their own childhood picnics. My grandmother would reminisce about how she met my grandfather at a picnic in that very meadow many years earlier. They exchanged shy smiles as the rest of the family teased them gently.

By late afternoon, when the sun dipped lower and cast golden light across the meadow, everyone became quiet, soaking in the calm. The oak's leaves rustled softly in the breeze, creating gentle shadows that danced across the blanket. Lying back, I'd watch clouds drifting by, listening to murmurs and quiet laughter around me.

We usually stayed until dusk approached. Gathering our things, we'd shake crumbs from the blanket, packing baskets that were much lighter now. The adults would slowly make their way toward the cars, still chatting, while we kids lingered behind, reluctant to leave the freedom of the open space and the comfort of the big oak.

Years later, those simple afternoons remain among my favorite memories. It wasn't anything extravagant—just family, sunshine, good food, and laughter. That old oak still stands tall, its branches spread wide, offering shade to new generations of families who might also find joy beneath its leaves.

Memory Prompts:

- Did you go on family picnics as a child?
- What food did you always hope would be in the basket?
- Do you recall a favorite park or countryside spot?

Conversation Starters:

- If you had a picnic today, where would you go?
- Do you enjoy picnics by the lake, the beach, or in a garden?
- What's your favorite picnic drink?

The Holiday Tablecloth

When holidays arrived, my mother would open the cabinet in our dining room and carefully take out the special tablecloth. It was soft cotton, ivory-colored, with delicate embroidery along the edges in shades of green, gold, and crimson. Over the years, it had developed a few stains that never washed out—a faded red wine blotch near the corner, a small drip of gravy near the center, and tiny wax marks from candles past. My mother would smooth her hand over the fabric, smiling fondly as each blemish brought a memory to life.

We used the tablecloth only on special days like Thanksgiving, Christmas, and Easter. Setting it out always felt like a ceremony. My sister and I were responsible for placing the dishes, the good china with silver edges, around the table. My mother would stand back, watching to make sure everything looked perfect.

The tablecloth wasn't only beautiful; it seemed to hold memories. When my grandmother visited, she'd touch a faded spot near her seat, laughing gently about a spilled glass from a holiday long past. My father liked to joke about the gravy stain, recalling my older brother's enthusiastic attempt to serve himself as a child. Each mark was tied to laughter, mistakes, forgiveness, and family warmth.

My father always sat at the head of the table, gently tapping a knife against his glass to quiet everyone when he gave thanks. His voice was deep and comforting, and as he spoke, eyes around the table glistened. My mother sat at the opposite end, smiling quietly as her family shared food and stories, the tablecloth beneath us absorbing every new memory.

Before eating, my grandmother would lead us in a short prayer, and we'd all say "amen" in unison. Immediately after, the conversations flowed, forks clinked, and plates passed from hand to hand. We'd fill our plates with slices of roasted turkey, creamy mashed potatoes, buttery rolls, and my aunt's famous green bean casserole. My favorite was always dessert—

pumpkin pie, dusted with cinnamon and topped with freshly whipped cream.

At the end of each meal, candles burned low, dripping tiny drops of wax onto the cloth. Rather than worry, my mother simply smiled and shrugged, saying, “Another memory for next time.”

Today, I have that tablecloth stored in my own dining room, folded neatly on a shelf, awaiting the next special occasion. Each time I spread it out, smoothing the wrinkles with my palms, the familiar imperfections stir warmth inside me. Now, my own family gathers around the tablecloth, adding new stains and memories. When my children accidentally spill something, they look at me nervously. But just like my mother, I smile and assure them it’s all part of our family's story.

That old tablecloth reminds me that family gatherings aren’t perfect. They're loud, messy, filled with mistakes and joy, and that’s exactly why they're precious. Each spot tells the story of the people who came before us, those who laughed, ate, loved, and left their mark for the next generation to remember.

Memory Prompts:

- Did your family have special dishes or table settings for holidays?
- Do you remember who always sat at the head of the table?
- Was there a song or prayer you shared before eating?

Conversation Starters:

- Do you prefer cooking for guests or being a guest?
- What’s your favorite holiday to celebrate with family?
- Do you enjoy decorating the table or the tree more?

Cousins in the Attic

On rainy afternoons when the grown-ups lingered over coffee downstairs, my cousins and I climbed the narrow wooden stairs to our grandparents' attic. A single bare bulb hung from the rafters, casting a dim glow over piles of forgotten boxes, dusty furniture, and mysterious treasures waiting to be uncovered.

The attic felt like another world, filled with whispers of the past. Old trunks lined the walls, their brass latches tarnished and covered in cobwebs. Our first task was always opening these trunks to see what hid inside. Carefully lifting the heavy lids, we found clothing from another time—hats decorated with faded silk ribbons, dresses with delicate lace, and suits smelling faintly of cedar. We giggled as we dressed up, posing and imitating the adults we'd seen in old black-and-white photographs.

Among the treasures were yellowed photo albums stacked on an old rocking chair. We'd sit cross-legged on the dusty floor, flipping pages carefully. The images captured scenes from our grandparents' youth: picnics, dances, and simple everyday moments that now seemed extraordinary. Every picture had a story we invented on the spot—dramatic tales of adventure, romance, and intrigue.

My cousin Tommy discovered an old telescope stored carefully in its leather case, and we took turns peering through its cloudy lens. Through the small attic window, we imagined distant ships sailing over rooftops and foreign lands hidden just beyond the horizon. Even though we saw only the neighbor's roof tiles and treetops, our imaginations carried us far beyond.

The most thrilling discovery came one day when we found a small, locked wooden chest hidden behind a stack of faded quilts. Determined to uncover its secrets, we searched every corner of the attic until we found a rusty key tucked in an old biscuit tin. With our hearts racing, we slowly opened the chest, expecting treasure or something magical. Inside were bundles of letters tied neatly with ribbon—love letters our grandparents exchanged decades ago. Although we couldn't fully understand their words, the handwriting alone spoke of romance and longing. Embarrassed but fascinated, we gently returned the letters to their resting place, carefully relocking the chest.

As evening approached and shadows stretched across the attic, we'd reluctantly put everything back where we found it. Before descending the stairs, we always promised each other that next time we'd explore even further, convinced there were still secrets hidden among the rafters.

Now, whenever my family gathers, my cousins and I still reminisce about those afternoons in the attic. Though decades have passed, we vividly recall how the dust tickled our noses, the creak of the floorboards beneath our feet, and how we imagined ourselves as explorers discovering new worlds.

The attic wasn't just a storage place; it was where our bonds were strengthened by shared secrets and adventures. Those afternoons exploring old trunks and dusty corners shaped who we became, reminding us that the best memories are often made in the simplest, most unexpected moments.

Memory Prompts:

- Did you ever explore an attic, cellar, or shed as a child?
- What forgotten objects fascinated you most?
- Did you play make-believe with cousins or siblings?

Conversation Starters:

- Would you rather explore an attic or a garden shed?
- What's the most surprising object you've ever found?
- Do you enjoy telling stories about your childhood home?

The Family Photo Day

When I was a child, family photo day was both exciting and a bit stressful. Early in the morning, my mother would pick outfits for each of us, neatly ironed and arranged on our beds. My brothers groaned when forced to wear buttoned shirts and ties, but my sister and I loved dressing up in our favorite dresses.

We gathered in the living room, a space my mother meticulously prepared the day before. The curtains were open just enough to let in soft, natural sunlight, and furniture was rearranged slightly so everyone could squeeze in. The photographer was usually my Uncle Ted, who owned a fancy camera he handled like a precious jewel.

As we lined up for the picture, the trouble always started. My little brother Jimmy never sat still for more than a minute, causing chaos as my father tried to hold him gently in place. My grandmother insisted on standing behind us, her hands resting warmly on our shoulders, quietly reminding everyone to smile.

Uncle Ted would fuss endlessly with his camera, adjusting dials, squinting into the lens, and repeatedly asking us to hold still. Someone always blinked at exactly the wrong moment, requiring another attempt. The longer it took, the harder it became not to burst into giggles, especially when our grandfather started whispering silly jokes just loud enough to set us laughing again.

After what seemed like hours—but was probably only a few minutes—Uncle Ted declared he had the perfect shot. We'd all rush to see the photo, eager to spot our faces on the small screen of his camera. My mother would sigh softly, relieved we'd finally gotten it right.

Once the formal photos were done, Uncle Ted encouraged us to relax, capturing candid moments. These were always my favorite. He'd snap pictures of my parents exchanging amused glances, my grandmother fixing my sister's hair, and my brothers wrestling playfully on the couch.

He always said these photos captured who we truly were, rather than stiff smiles and carefully arranged poses.

Later, after dinner, we'd gather around a box of older family photographs, digging out previous years' pictures and comparing how everyone had grown and changed. My grandfather would tease my dad about the increasing gray hairs visible in each new photo, while my mother gently touched pictures of relatives who had since passed, smiling wistfully as she shared stories about them.

Today, these family photos hang proudly on my own walls. They're reminders of our shared history, a record of how we've grown together through the years. Even the silly or imperfect photos hold meaning now—the crooked ties, messy hair, and awkward expressions make me smile whenever I look at them.

Those days taught me the importance of capturing small, seemingly ordinary moments. Years later, it's clear to me that photo day was more than just creating images. It was about gathering together, sharing laughter and love, and creating memories to last beyond our lifetimes.

Memory Prompts:

- Did you remember taking family photos as a child?
- Did you have a favorite outfit for special occasions?
- Can you recall looking through old photo albums?

Conversation Starters:

- Do you enjoy being in photos or taking them?
- Which family photo is your favorite to look at?
- Would you prefer a formal portrait or a candid snapshot?

Grandpa's Garden Bench

After family dinners at my grandparents' house, I often found myself outside in their backyard, sitting on a weathered wooden bench beside my grandfather. The bench stood next to his garden, overlooking neat rows of tomato plants, beans climbing wooden stakes, and marigolds planted at the borders to keep pests away. Grandpa would lean back with a soft sigh, relaxing after the lively conversations of the dining table.

It was quiet outside except for the soft hum of crickets and occasional laughter drifting from inside the house. The scent of freshly watered soil and tomato plants mixed in the air, familiar and comforting. Grandpa would reach down, plucking a cherry tomato from the vine, popping it into his mouth. He'd always offer one to me, and we'd savor their sweet, warm flavor together.

On that bench, Grandpa told stories about his younger days. I remember him speaking softly about his time working in the city, riding crowded buses to his job in a small shop. He described busy streets, noisy cars, and a life very different from his peaceful garden. When I asked if he missed the excitement, he'd smile gently and shake his head, saying nothing compared to the quiet of his own yard.

As the evening stretched on, Grandpa shared advice he'd learned over his lifetime, wisdom wrapped in simple, clear words. He often talked about patience, especially when growing vegetables. "Plants teach you about life," he'd say. "They don't rush. They need sun, rain, and plenty of patience—just like people."

Those evenings on the garden bench gave us time to connect in a quiet, personal way. Once, I asked him how he knew Grandma was "the one." He smiled shyly, his cheeks coloring a little. "When I met her," he said softly, "everything else seemed less important. She made simple moments feel special." I glanced back at the house, where Grandma stood at the kitchen window, washing dishes and occasionally looking out to check on us. I knew exactly what he meant.

As the sky turned shades of pink and lavender, Grandpa often became quieter. We'd sit in comfortable silence, watching fireflies float lazily across the grass. He'd point out constellations emerging in the deepening sky, telling me their names. Even today, when I look up at those same stars, his voice echoes softly in my memory.

Years later, when Grandpa passed away, the bench became even more precious. Though weathered and cracked with age, no one considered replacing it. It felt as though part of him remained there, waiting patiently to share another evening in the garden.

Now, when family gatherings wind down, I find myself drawn back to Grandpa's bench. Sitting there brings comfort, warmth, and countless memories of conversations shared beneath stars and amid thriving vegetables. Grandpa's lessons still guide me: slow down, enjoy quiet moments, and savor the sweetness in life.

Memory Prompts:

- Did someone in your family enjoy gardening?
- Do you remember sitting outside with relatives?
- What lessons did you learn from your grandparents?

Conversation Starters:

- Do you enjoy flowers or vegetable gardens more?
- If you could plant one tree, what would it be?
- Do you like spending time in the garden today?

The Family Radio Hour

In our house, evenings had their own comforting routine. After dinner, we'd clear the table, wash dishes, and settle into the living room to gather around the radio. This was a nightly tradition we rarely missed, and everyone had their own favorite seat. My father sat in his big, cushioned chair, my mother settled onto the sofa with her knitting, and we children sprawled on the soft carpet, eager to hear the program that would soon fill the room with music and stories.

The old radio sat proudly on a sturdy wooden stand, its fabric-covered speaker humming softly as it warmed up. My father carefully turned the dials, adjusting the signal until static gave way to the clear, familiar voice of our favorite broadcaster. His deep, calm tone felt like part of our family, an invisible guest welcomed warmly each night.

Most evenings, we enjoyed music programs, tapping our feet gently in rhythm or quietly humming along. My mother's knitting needles clicked softly, almost in harmony with the melodies drifting from the speaker. Occasionally, my parents would share a brief, knowing glance, reminding us how certain songs connected them to memories from their youth.

Other nights, the program featured radio dramas. These stories pulled us into faraway worlds filled with heroes, villains, and adventures. We listened intently, eyes wide, imaginations fully engaged. On thrilling episodes, I would inch closer to my siblings, gripping a pillow, our hearts racing as characters escaped danger at the last moment. During funny scenes, laughter filled the room, bouncing off the walls as we giggled and repeated our favorite lines.

As much as I loved the stories, the best part was often the moments between segments. During commercials, my father would turn the volume down, and we'd chat briefly about the day or the characters we'd just heard. It was a chance to share our own thoughts, sometimes predicting the outcome or debating our favorite moments.

Occasionally, news updates broke into our nightly program. My father would sit forward slightly, turning the dial louder, listening carefully to events happening far from our cozy living room. Afterward, he'd explain the news in simple words, helping us understand the world beyond our front door.

When the show ended, the broadcaster wished listeners a peaceful night, his voice gently fading into soft music. My father clicked off the radio, the sudden quiet feeling oddly warm. My mother would gather her knitting, gently nudging us to bed.

Many years later, I still clearly recall those radio evenings. We didn't realize at the time how precious those shared hours would become. The simple act of listening together connected us, creating memories that linger warmly even today.

Sometimes, late at night, I find myself switching on the radio, listening to music or news, recalling those cozy family evenings. Though radios look different now and broadcasts have changed, the comfort remains. For me, the radio will always be tied to the love, warmth, and joy of family gathered closely, sharing stories and music in the gentle glow of home.

Memory Prompts:

- Did your family have a regular evening routine together?
- Do you remember a favorite show or program?
- Who usually chose what to listen to?

Conversation Starters:

- Do you prefer music, stories, or news on the radio?
- Would you enjoy listening to an old radio play again?
- Do you still follow the news on TV, radio, or online?

The Family Quilt

When winter came and evenings grew colder, my mother would bring out our family quilt from a cedar chest at the foot of her bed. She unfolded it carefully, smoothing its soft patches of fabric with gentle hands. Each colorful square carried a memory, stitched together from worn clothing belonging to generations of relatives.

I loved tracing the quilt's squares with my fingertips. My mother would sit beside me, pointing out pieces of fabric and telling stories about them. "This plaid was from your grandfather's favorite shirt," she'd say. "He wore it fishing every summer." Next to it was a square cut from my grandmother's kitchen apron, faded from years of baking pies and holiday treats.

There were squares made from dresses my mother wore as a young girl, faded pastels of floral patterns. Near them was fabric from my father's old work shirts, still strong and sturdy. My favorite pieces were those taken from pajamas my siblings and I had outgrown, soft and comforting even now. Touching each patch brought back memories of bedtime stories, laughter, and whispered secrets late at night.

The quilt itself was sewn by my grandmother, who worked quietly each evening until her eyes grew tired. She collected pieces from everyone in the family, carefully matching colors and patterns to reflect our personalities. When she presented the finished quilt at a family gathering one winter, tears filled many eyes around the room, moved by her thoughtfulness and care.

That quilt became a comforting presence in our home, especially on snowy nights when the wind whistled outside and frost formed patterns on windowpanes. We'd gather around the fireplace, pulling the quilt close, sharing warmth as much from family closeness as from the soft fabric.

My grandmother's quilt traveled with us through time, spreading across beds, draping over couches, and wrapping around shoulders. When someone felt ill, it provided comfort and warmth. If there was sadness or worry, the quilt was a gentle reminder of family bonds, stitched firmly together.

Over the years, the colors faded slightly, and edges frayed from frequent use, but we cherished it even more. My mother taught me to mend small tears, carefully choosing thread to match each patch. We spent quiet afternoons sitting side by side, working slowly and patiently, my mother recalling stories that matched the squares we repaired.

Today, the family quilt is passed down to me. Each winter, I remove it carefully from storage, breathing in the familiar scent of cedar and memories. I share its stories with my own children, telling them about relatives they never met but who live on in fabric and thread. Like me, they trace their fingers across faded squares, imagining scenes from our family's past.

I hope someday, they'll share this quilt with their own families, weaving new memories into its patches. Through every stitch and each lovingly chosen square, the quilt reminds us that families are connected not only by blood but by shared experiences, care, and warmth handed down through generations.

Memory Prompts:

- Did someone in your family enjoy sewing or quilting?
- Do you remember an old blanket or heirloom from home?
- What clothes or fabrics remind you of loved ones?

Conversation Starters:

- Do you prefer handmade or store-bought gifts?
- If you could design a quilt, what colors would you choose?
- Do you enjoy crafts or watching others create them?

Voices at the Dinner Table

Dinner at my childhood home was rarely quiet. Our family meals were filled with lively conversations, quick jokes, and the warm sound of laughter echoing from every corner of the kitchen. Even before we sat down, voices overlapped cheerfully, creating a familiar hum of excitement around the table.

My mother cooked hearty meals that seemed simple but tasted delicious: roast chicken with crisp potatoes, creamy casseroles, and fluffy biscuits hot from the oven. Everyone eagerly took their seats, chatting happily while passing plates and serving dishes. It always felt crowded around that table, elbows brushing and knees occasionally bumping, but I loved the coziness of it all.

My father typically started the conversation, asking us about our day or sharing something interesting he had heard. He had a way of making even ordinary details sound exciting, holding our attention as he recounted a funny encounter or small mishap at work. Soon, everyone joined in, adding their own stories and playful comments.

My older brother, James, was the family comedian. He'd imitate teachers or neighbors, exaggerating their voices and gestures until we doubled over laughing. Sometimes, he would quietly toss a silly remark into a serious conversation, causing my mother to feign annoyance before breaking into a smile herself.

My sister, always dramatic, shared stories about her friends and classmates with animated expressions and energetic gestures. She captivated everyone with her ability to turn small incidents into amusing tales. Even our parents chuckled at her theatrical descriptions, shaking their heads affectionately.

Occasionally, the room grew briefly quiet as we savored the food. But soon enough, someone would start humming a tune, often sparking an impromptu sing-along. None of us had particularly good voices, but that never stopped us from singing loudly and cheerfully, forks and spoons tapping rhythmically against plates.

One evening, my grandfather joined us for dinner. Usually quiet and reserved, he listened thoughtfully to the conversations around him. When my brother told one of his funniest jokes, my grandfather suddenly broke into laughter, a deep, hearty sound we'd never heard before. Surprised, we all turned toward him, then joined in, the table shaking gently with shared joy.

Those lively dinners brought us closer together in ways we didn't fully understand until much later. It wasn't just the food that nourished us, but also the laughter, stories, and warmth exchanged every night. Even small disagreements ended quickly, resolved by humor or a gentle tease.

Now, whenever I find myself at a silent dinner table, I remember those noisy, joyful evenings from my childhood. I realize how those family meals shaped my understanding of love, comfort, and connection. Each voice, each laugh, and each silly song created memories that still make me smile today.

In my own family now, I try to recreate that same warmth at dinner, encouraging stories, jokes, and laughter. And when the conversation grows loud, and laughter fills the room, I feel grateful for those dinners of my youth that taught me the true meaning of family.

Memory Prompts:

- Did your family eat together every night?
- Do you remember the funniest dinner conversation you had?
- Who always made everyone laugh at the table?

Conversation Starters:

- Do you prefer quiet meals or lively gatherings?
- What makes a meal feel special to you?
- Would you rather eat indoors or outdoors with family?

The Annual Family Trip to the Fair

Each summer, when the fair arrived in town, excitement buzzed through our house. Early in the morning, my siblings and I woke up to the anticipation of bright lights, colorful rides, and delicious smells drifting through the air. We would quickly eat breakfast, barely tasting our toast and juice, impatient to set out for the fairgrounds.

My father would park near the entrance, and as soon as we opened the car doors, the lively sounds surrounded us. Music played cheerfully from distant rides, vendors called out enthusiastically, and laughter echoed from every direction. Immediately, the sweet scent of cotton candy and buttery popcorn filled our senses, drawing us toward the bustling midway.

Each family member had their favorite attraction. My sister loved the carousel, her eyes lighting up as the painted horses circled gracefully to cheerful music. My brother preferred games, tossing rings or shooting water pistols to win stuffed animals or plastic toys. As for me, I always made a beeline to the Ferris wheel. It towered impressively over the fair, promising beautiful views from the top.

We stayed together, exploring each stand and attraction as a group, taking turns choosing what to do next. My mother enjoyed looking at homemade crafts in the exhibition hall, admiring quilts, jams, and intricately knitted sweaters. My father sampled the fair's foods, happily buying funnel cakes and roasted peanuts to share.

One memorable year, my grandmother joined us. Though hesitant at first, she bravely climbed onto the Ferris wheel beside me. As we rose slowly higher, her eyes widened in surprise and delight. From the top, we gazed across our small town, marveling at rooftops, fields, and streets stretching far into the distance. She squeezed my hand gently, whispering that the view reminded her of childhood adventures she hadn't thought of in years.

As evening approached, colored lights on rides began to glow brighter, sparkling like stars against the darkening sky. The sounds of the fair softened, becoming a comforting backdrop to our conversations. With tired feet and happy hearts, we'd pause for treats—ice cream cones melting quickly in the summer heat, or crunchy caramel apples that left our fingers sticky.

Before leaving, we always visited the small souvenir stand. We picked out tiny treasures: postcards featuring scenes from the fair, miniature toy animals, or balloons that bobbed cheerfully above our heads. Clutching our souvenirs, we walked slowly back to the car, chatting happily about our favorite moments from the day.

Looking back, the annual fair brought more than just fun. It was a tradition that connected us, year after year, through shared excitement and simple joys. Even as we grew older, our love for the fair never faded. It became part of our family story, weaving together memories of childhood wonder and the warmth of being together.

Now, whenever I hear carnival music or smell the sweet aroma of cotton candy, I'm transported back to those joyful summer days. I see my family laughing together beneath bright lights, feel the gentle sway of the Ferris wheel, and smile warmly, thankful for traditions that endure.

Memory Prompts:

- Did your family attend local fairs or festivals?
- Do you remember your favorite fairground treat?
- What ride did you enjoy the most as a child?

Conversation Starters:

- Would you rather ride the carousel or the Ferris wheel?
- Do you enjoy music, games, or food more at fairs?
- What would you bring home as a souvenir?

Chapter 3: Love & Companionship

Throughout life, love often reveals itself quietly, in simple, everyday gestures. This chapter celebrates those moments—the warmth of a familiar hand reaching out to hold yours, an evening spent swaying slowly to a favorite song, or the laughter shared when two people huddle beneath one umbrella to escape the rain. Love might also show itself in rediscovered letters tucked away in drawers, gentle conversations on a porch swing at sunset, or even a shy proposal whispered under a starry sky. The stories ahead capture how companionship enriches ordinary days, making them extraordinary in subtle ways. As you read, allow yourself the pleasure of recalling the special bonds you've formed over the years. Maybe you'll be reminded of someone who made your heart flutter, a friendship that unexpectedly blossomed into romance, or simply the comforting presence of someone who knew your stories by heart. These narratives might also stir memories of weddings, joyful gatherings, or a song playing from a jukebox in a favorite café. Love, after all, isn't only found in grand gestures but also in moments quietly shared and gently treasured. Let these stories remind you of the relationships that have made your journey through life so rewarding.

The Letter in the Drawer

Eleanor was always practical, organizing each day around simple routines. But this morning, while sorting through clothes to donate, her fingers brushed against something hidden at the back of her dresser drawer.

She gently pulled out a faded blue envelope, her breath catching as she recognized the elegant handwriting. "For Eleanor," it read, sending her heart back to a long-ago summer when life felt fresh and every choice seemed full of possibility. Slowly, she opened the letter, careful not to tear its delicate edges.

"Dearest Eleanor," it began, instantly transporting her to that year she turned nineteen. Memories surfaced vividly—lazy afternoons spent walking beside the quiet river with William, sharing secret smiles and whispered dreams.

He wrote of his feelings, shyly confessed in ink because words had always come easier to him that way. William's tender sentences described a future he hoped to share, a future she had once imagined too. Eleanor remembered his hopeful gaze the day she gently told him her plans would take her elsewhere, a gentle refusal she had made with a heavy heart.

Reading his words now brought a tender ache. William had married soon afterward, and Eleanor had found happiness along another path. But holding the letter today reminded her of the sweetness of first love, pure and untouched by the practical realities of life. She realized this single sheet of paper held more than just words—it held a youthful innocence she rarely revisited.

Eleanor carefully folded the letter, tucking it back in its envelope. She smiled softly at photographs on her dresser: images of a life she'd built carefully, deliberately. Her husband smiled from one frame, his gaze as warm as the day they married. Beside him stood their children, now grown, faces filled with laughter.

Love, she reflected, had grown with her. It wasn't always romantic or passionate; sometimes it was quiet strength, steady hands, and whispered support. Each love was precious, each memory shaping who she had become.

Closing the drawer gently, she decided the letter should remain there. Someday, perhaps, her granddaughter might uncover it and ask about the story hidden inside. Eleanor knew she'd enjoy telling her about William, the letter, and the way life had gently led her forward.

Stepping outside into the sunlight, Eleanor felt unexpectedly lighter. Maybe today she'd write her own letter—not about youthful promises, but about quiet gratitude. She'd share the small joys that filled her days, hoping to pass on some of the happiness that had grown in her heart.

In the warmth of the morning sun, Eleanor smiled. The practical errands she'd planned could wait a little longer. Today was for reflection, for quiet appreciation of all the love she'd known—both old and new—and the letter that had reminded her how beautifully life's paths could weave together.

Memory Prompts:

- Did you ever receive a love letter?
- How did people in your time express affection?
- Do you remember a meaningful keepsake you saved?

Conversation Starters:

- Do you prefer writing letters or making phone calls?
- What's the most thoughtful gift you've ever received?
- If someone wrote you a letter today, what would you like it to say?

Dancing Shoes by the Radio

After supper, Evelyn cleared away the dishes, humming softly. Henry lingered at the table, folding the evening paper, pretending not to notice the tender melody escaping from his wife's lips. He knew that tune. It always started quietly, building into something irresistible.

"Henry," Evelyn called gently, stepping into the living room. "Turn on the radio, would you?"

He rose slowly, as he always did, his knees creaking softly as he moved. At the old wooden console radio, Henry twisted the familiar dial, searching for the station that played the songs they had always loved. Static crackled briefly, then gave way to the warm, soothing voice of Nat King Cole. Evelyn smiled, extending a hand toward her husband.

"Dance with me?"

Henry chuckled, shaking his head gently. But even as he pretended reluctance, he was already moving toward her. Their steps were slower these days, but they still held the same grace, born from decades spent learning the rhythm of each other's movements. They glided slowly across the worn living room carpet, their feet tracing patterns known only to them. Evelyn's eyes sparkled with joy, reflecting memories of Saturday night dances at the old community hall, where Henry had first asked her to dance. He'd been so nervous then, fumbling his words as she patiently waited, smiling kindly until he found his courage. That night had been the beginning of a tradition, a simple joy they continued to cherish, even as time slipped quietly forward. Tonight, surrounded by the warmth of their home, they danced again. The radio's soft music filled the room, mixing gently with the evening breeze drifting through the curtains. Evelyn rested her head lightly on Henry's shoulder, breathing in the familiar scent of his aftershave, comforted by the steady rhythm of his heartbeat.

"Remember that summer evening at the lake?" Henry asked softly, his voice rich with nostalgia.

"How could I forget?" Evelyn laughed gently. "You hummed the whole evening because you forgot the radio."

"It worked, didn't it?" Henry teased.

"It always did," she replied warmly.

The melody on the radio shifted to a familiar waltz, carrying them deeper into the sweet haze of memory. Henry tightened his embrace slightly, careful not to press too hard against Evelyn's back, mindful of the years that had shaped their steps.

They danced on, the worries of the day forgotten. Each gentle sway was a quiet affirmation of the life they'd built together—a simple life filled with quiet laughter, gentle gestures, and countless dances shared in this very room. As the song faded into silence, Henry and Evelyn slowed to a gentle stop. He kissed her forehead softly, their fingers still intertwined.

"Thank you for the dance, dear," he whispered, meeting her eyes with a tenderness that had only deepened over the years.

"Anytime," Evelyn replied softly. Her voice was filled with the quiet certainty that there would always be another song, another dance, another chance to hold each other close.

Outside, the evening settled into a gentle darkness, but within their home, warmth lingered—carried softly on the notes of an old melody, waiting patiently for the next time they turned on the radio and began to move, together once more.

Memory Prompts:

- Did you enjoy dancing when you were younger?
- Do you remember a favorite song to dance to?
- Who was your favorite dance partner?

Conversation Starters:

- Do you prefer slow dances or lively ones?
- If you could dance anywhere, where would it be?
- What kind of music makes you want to move?

The Park Bench Meeting

George visited the park nearly every afternoon, usually with a newspaper tucked beneath his arm and some stale bread for the ducks. His routine was simple. He'd settle onto his favorite bench near the pond, nod politely at passersby, and watch life quietly pass along the walking path.

One sunny day, however, George found someone already occupying his usual bench. A woman with silver hair was seated comfortably, tossing breadcrumbs toward the eager ducks splashing close by. She looked up, sensing his hesitation, and offered a friendly smile.

“Plenty of room,” she said warmly, shifting slightly to one side.

George nodded gratefully and sat down. They fed the ducks quietly, sharing the comfortable silence that often grows between strangers enjoying a peaceful afternoon.

“It’s a lovely spot, isn’t it?” she finally offered, glancing sideways with a gentle smile.

“It certainly is,” George agreed. “Been coming here for years.”

“Me too,” she replied, eyes twinkling. “Strange we’ve never crossed paths before.”

They both laughed softly, surprised and amused. Soon, small talk grew into deeper conversation, their laughter carrying across the pond as they shared stories from their lives. George learned her name was Margaret. She had lived just blocks away from him for years. Her husband had passed away, leaving her seeking quiet moments outdoors. George nodded sympathetically, sharing how he'd lost his wife a few years earlier, how the bench had become a quiet place to reflect and remember.

Days passed into weeks, and soon their casual meetings turned into an anticipated daily event. Margaret brought homemade cookies, wrapped neatly in wax paper. George brought fresh bread from the bakery instead of stale crumbs. Together they talked about everything, from gardening tips to grandchildren's birthdays. Each afternoon spent chatting on the bench became a bright spot in their days, blending easily into friendship.

Months later, Margaret hesitated before speaking one afternoon. "George," she began softly, "I was wondering if you might like to join me for dinner sometime?"

George smiled, a bit surprised, but he realized how natural it felt. "I'd like that very much," he replied warmly.

That first dinner led to many more shared meals and pleasant evenings. Soon their friendship grew stronger, gently transforming into a love neither had anticipated but warmly welcomed. Their grown children teased them gently, delighted by the unexpected turn their parents' lives had taken.

On a mild spring afternoon, exactly one year after their first meeting, George took Margaret's hand as they sat on their favorite bench. "Funny how life surprises you, isn't it?" he asked softly.

Margaret squeezed his hand affectionately. "Best surprise of my life," she answered.

They sat quietly then, grateful for chance encounters and simple conversations. Around them, ducks quacked softly, children laughed, and the breeze rustled gently through the trees. But for George and Margaret, it was enough to sit together, comfortable and content, quietly grateful for the afternoon that had changed everything.

Memory Prompts:

- Did you ever meet someone special by chance?
- Do you recall a park or public place you visited often?
- Have you ever had a friendship turn into something more?

Conversation Starters:

- Do you enjoy people-watching in public places?
- If you could meet someone new today, what would you ask first?
- Do you prefer quiet moments together or lively outings?

The Shared Umbrella

Anna had always loved rainy days. She enjoyed the gentle rhythm of raindrops tapping windows, forming patterns that blurred softly against the glass. But today, caught unexpectedly without her umbrella, Anna stood beneath a shop awning, watching the rain pour and wondering how she'd get home without becoming soaked.

As she waited, footsteps approached. A young man carrying a small blue umbrella stopped nearby, glancing out at the heavy downpour.

“Quite a storm,” he remarked with a gentle smile.

Anna nodded, returning the smile. “Of all days, I forgot my umbrella.”

He laughed lightly, adjusting his grip. “Usually, that's my luck too. Today, somehow, I remembered.” After a pause, he glanced toward her. “Which way are you heading?”

“Just a few blocks down Elm Street,” Anna replied, gesturing into the misty distance.

“Me too,” he said warmly. “We could share mine if you’d like.”

Anna hesitated only briefly before smiling gratefully. “Thank you. That’s very kind.”

They stepped carefully into the rain, shoulders brushing beneath the tiny umbrella. Drops splashed onto their shoes as the wind tilted the canopy sideways, making them laugh softly.

“Sorry,” he said quickly, trying to steady the umbrella.

“It’s fine,” Anna reassured him. “A little water won't hurt.”

“I’m David,” he introduced himself as they moved along the slick sidewalk.

“Anna,” she replied, glancing sideways, noticing the warmth in his eyes despite the gray afternoon.

Conversation flowed naturally as they walked. David spoke of his work at a local bookstore, making Anna laugh with stories of quirky customers.

Anna shared tales of teaching third grade, describing the humorous antics of her students.

When they reached Elm Street, Anna pointed toward a small, cozy house. “This is my place,” she told him softly.

David stopped, smiling warmly. “Well, it was nice meeting you, Anna.”

“Thanks again for rescuing me from the rain,” she replied.

“My pleasure,” David said, lingering a moment. Then he added quickly, “Maybe we could meet again sometime, preferably on a sunnier day?”

Anna felt herself blush, nodding gently. “I’d like that.”

“Great,” he replied brightly. “I'll be at the bookstore tomorrow afternoon if you want to stop by.”

“See you then,” she promised, stepping toward her porch.

David waved briefly before turning, disappearing slowly into the rainy mist. Anna watched from her doorway, smiling softly. Inside, warmth filled her chest, grateful for the unexpected storm and the kindness of a stranger.

Tomorrow promised sunshine, a new friendship, and perhaps something even sweeter than the rain she’d always loved.

Memory Prompts:

- Do you remember being caught in the rain?
- Did you ever walk home with someone special after school or work?
- What was your favorite kind of rainy-day activity?

Conversation Starters:

- Do you like rainy days or sunny days better?
- Would you rather walk in the rain or stay cozy indoors?
- What’s your favorite rainy-day song or movie?

A Proposal Under the Stars

When Paul suggested a nighttime walk along the lakeshore, Mary agreed without hesitation. It had been a warm day, and now the cool breeze drifting off the water made the evening perfect for strolling together. They walked hand in hand, comfortable in their quiet companionship, listening to the gentle lap of waves against the shore.

The lake was calm, reflecting the scattered stars overhead. Mary glanced upward, sighing softly. "Isn't it beautiful?" she whispered, her voice filled with awe.

Paul smiled warmly. "Yes, it certainly is." But his eyes weren't fixed on the sky; they rested gently on Mary's face, softly illuminated by moonlight.

They stopped at their favorite spot beneath an old willow tree whose branches touched the surface of the water. Paul reached into his pocket, pulling out a small velvet box that he'd carried for weeks, waiting for the right moment.

Mary turned to find Paul watching her closely, his eyes gentle yet serious.

"What is it?" she asked quietly, her heartbeat quickening as she recognized something special unfolding.

Paul opened the box slowly, revealing a delicate ring, its diamond catching the moonlight softly.

"Mary," he began gently, "you've filled my days with joy, laughter, and kindness. You've been my best friend and the greatest part of my life. Would you do me the honor of becoming my wife?"

Mary's eyes widened, her heart fluttering with surprise and happiness. A joyful smile spread across her face, and tears glistened softly in her eyes.

"Oh, Paul, of course I will," she said, her voice trembling slightly. "Nothing would make me happier."

Paul took the ring carefully from the box and slid it gently onto her finger. Mary admired it, feeling an overwhelming wave of love and excitement.

Paul pulled her close, embracing her gently beneath the endless expanse of stars.

They stood quietly, savoring the beauty of this moment, feeling connected not just to each other, but to the stillness of the lake, the whispering branches, and the quiet glow of the night sky.

Eventually, Paul broke the silence. "Did you ever imagine we would be here one day?"

Mary laughed softly, shaking her head. "Maybe not exactly like this," she replied. "But in my heart, I hoped."

"Me too," Paul admitted, squeezing her hand warmly.

They turned slowly back toward the path, beginning the quiet walk home, their future ahead full of possibilities. Above them, the stars seemed brighter, as if sharing their happiness.

As they reached their doorstep, Mary paused, gazing upward again.

"What is it?" Paul asked gently, following her eyes.

"I was just thinking," she answered softly, "that every time I look up at these stars, I'll remember tonight."

Paul nodded, smiling warmly. "Me too," he promised. "Always."

Hand in hand, they stepped inside, hearts full, knowing this night would forever remain a gentle memory, guiding their love like stars lighting their way home.

Memory Prompts:

- Do you remember where you were proposed to, or a special proposal you witnessed?
- What starry nights from your past stand out?
- Did you have a favorite romantic spot growing up?

Conversation Starters:

- Do you prefer a simple proposal or a grand gesture?
- What’s the most beautiful night sky you’ve seen?
- Do you enjoy stargazing with others?

The Wedding Quilt

Grace smoothed her hand gently over the quilt spread across her bed. Soft fabric squares, stitched together by careful hands decades ago, formed a patchwork filled with stories. Each piece carried memories, given lovingly by friends and family when she married Daniel.

The quilt had arrived the day before their wedding, wrapped neatly with a ribbon. Grace remembered the excitement as she unwrapped it, her mother standing nearby, watching proudly.

"It's tradition," her mother had explained softly, eyes glistening. "Every square is from someone who loves you both."

Now, years later, Grace traced one particular patch, smiling softly. It was pale blue, faded now but still beautiful, a square from Daniel's grandmother. She had sewn it with steady hands, wishing them happiness. Nearby was a floral square, bright and cheerful, crafted by Grace's best friend. Next to that, a soft green piece from her sister, stitched with tiny, careful stitches. Grace's fingers moved from square to square, each one sparking gentle memories. She thought of evenings spent wrapped in this quilt beside Daniel, planning their future, speaking softly about dreams and hopes. It had comforted them through chilly winters, warmed their newborn daughter, and now held the stories of their grandchildren's laughter.

Hearing footsteps approach, Grace turned to see Daniel entering the room. He paused, smiling warmly as he noticed the quilt.

"It still looks beautiful," he remarked gently, coming to stand beside her.

"It does," Grace agreed, smiling softly. "It's held up well, hasn't it?"

"Like us," Daniel said, eyes twinkling affectionately.

Grace laughed quietly, squeezing his hand. "Do you remember how we first used it?"

Daniel nodded, chuckling softly. "Our first winter together. That tiny apartment was freezing."

"Yet we never felt cold," Grace added warmly, "thanks to this."

They stood quietly together, reflecting on shared years and the memories captured within fabric squares. Each piece of the quilt was a small reminder of friendships and family, of the love that had strengthened them through life's changes.

Grace thought of their daughter, newly married, starting her own journey. Soon, she would receive a quilt of her own, stitched with love, carrying the hopes of another generation.

"Do you think Emily's quilt will mean as much to her as ours does to us?" Grace wondered softly.

Daniel smiled gently. "I hope so. Maybe even more."

Grace nodded thoughtfully. "Perhaps we should add a square from our quilt to hers, pass on some of our happiness."

Daniel squeezed her hand gently. "Perfect idea."

They stood a moment longer, savoring the quiet. Around them, the house was peaceful, filled with reminders of a life shared. The quilt on the bed was more than fabric; it was their story, carefully preserved through the years. Grace folded the quilt neatly, smoothing it carefully. Tomorrow they would choose the square to pass down, continuing a tradition of love that connected their past to their daughter's future. Quietly, they left the room, hearts full, knowing that the simple stitches of a quilt could hold so much joy, warmth, and hope for the days to come.

Memory Prompts:

- Do you recall a handmade wedding gift you received or gave?
- Did your family have a tradition for weddings?
- Do you remember attending a wedding that felt very special?

Conversation Starters:

- Do you prefer small weddings or big celebrations?
- What makes a wedding memorable to you?
- Do you enjoy dancing at weddings?

The Porch Swing Evenings

Helen and Frank sat quietly on their porch swing, gently swaying as the evening settled around them. The day's warmth lingered pleasantly, fading into a soft, golden twilight. From their spot, they could see neighbors walking dogs, children chasing fireflies, and hear distant laughter drifting through the summer air.

This porch swing had always been their favorite place. It was where they shared quiet talks, enjoyed gentle silences, and watched countless sunsets paint the sky. Tonight, Helen leaned softly against Frank, listening to the creak of chains moving slowly above them.

"Do you remember our first evening out here?" Frank asked quietly, a nostalgic smile forming.

Helen laughed softly. "How could I forget? You spent hours putting this swing together. I thought you might give up."

Frank chuckled. "Nearly did. But I knew how much you wanted it."

They both smiled, each recalling the younger versions of themselves—excited to fill their new home with warmth and happy memories. Over the years, the swing had become a comforting constant, a gentle rhythm behind their lives.

"What's your favorite memory out here?" Helen asked softly, curious.

Frank thought carefully, eyes twinkling. "There are many. But maybe the evening our granddaughter took her first steps on this porch. Do you remember?" Helen smiled warmly, nodding. "She stood right by the railing, determined as anything."

"And then she walked straight toward you," Frank continued, chuckling fondly. "She knew you'd catch her."

Helen squeezed his hand lightly. "I always would."

They fell comfortably silent again, watching as daylight faded into deeper shades of purple and blue. The quiet around them was familiar, comforting, filled with countless evenings just like this one.

"I think that's what I love most about this swing," Helen finally said. "The way it holds all our memories, every story we've shared right here."

Frank nodded thoughtfully. "Even the quiet ones."

Especially the quiet ones, Helen thought. They had always understood each other best in moments like these, when words weren't needed.

Slowly, the porch lights around their neighborhood flickered on, casting soft pools of yellow along the street. Crickets began their nightly song, blending gently into the background.

"Do you think our children will have a spot like this one day?" Helen wondered aloud, picturing their busy lives.

Frank smiled warmly. "I hope so. Everyone needs a peaceful place to sit, remember, and rest."

Helen sighed contentedly, leaning closer. "I'm grateful we have ours."

They swayed gently, enjoying the comfort of each other's presence. Around them, the night deepened, stars appearing slowly overhead.

Eventually, Frank spoke softly, breaking their thoughtful silence. "I think I'll never grow tired of these evenings."

Helen smiled, eyes closed gently. "Me neither. There's nothing better."

As darkness settled fully, they continued to sit together, quietly sharing the joy of simple moments, secure in the knowledge that tomorrow would bring another peaceful evening right here on their beloved porch swing.

Memory Prompts:

- Did you ever have a favorite place to sit and talk?
- What did you enjoy doing with your partner or friends in the evening?
- Do you remember a view that always calmed you?

Conversation Starters:

- Do you prefer morning sunrises or evening sunsets?
- What makes a place feel peaceful to you?
- Would you rather share stories or sit quietly with someone you love?

The Long Walk Home

After the town's annual harvest festival, Martha found herself chatting with James, a neighbor she'd known casually for years. They had volunteered at the same booth, handing out freshly baked pies and enjoying the festive atmosphere. As the evening ended, they realized they were both walking in the same direction home.

"Would you mind some company?" James asked warmly, tipping his hat slightly.

"I'd be delighted," Martha replied, smiling gently.

They started their walk down the quiet, tree-lined street. The distant sounds of the festival faded slowly behind them, replaced by the soothing hum of crickets and the occasional rustle of leaves beneath their feet. The crisp night air felt refreshing after the day's excitement.

At first, their conversation was simple, touching lightly on the festival and friendly neighborhood gossip. Soon, however, their words turned deeper, more personal. Martha learned about James's childhood in the countryside, and he listened with interest as she shared memories of her summers spent at her grandmother's farm. They both laughed recalling how different the town had been when they were younger. James described how he'd raced bicycles down these same streets, carefree and adventurous. Martha smiled warmly, remembering quieter days spent reading beneath the large oak trees lining their path.

As they walked, their pace slowed, each of them appreciating the unexpected ease of their conversation. James glanced sideways, noticing the gentle way Martha's eyes crinkled when she laughed, and Martha found herself drawn to his thoughtful manner and quiet kindness.

Reaching the small bridge over the town's creek, they paused, leaning gently against the railing, looking out over moonlit water. Martha sighed softly, enjoying the peaceful moment.

"It's beautiful here at night," she said quietly, her voice filled with genuine appreciation.

James nodded thoughtfully. "Funny how you can pass by something every day and never really see it until you stop and share it with someone."

Martha smiled warmly. "Exactly."

They stood quietly together, savoring the simplicity of sharing a familiar view through new eyes. After a moment, James turned toward Martha, a slight hesitation in his voice. "You know, it's strange," he began, "we've known each other all these years, but tonight feels like the first time we've truly talked."

Martha met his gaze gently. "I feel the same. It's funny how one evening can change things."

James nodded, encouraged by her words. "Maybe we shouldn't wait until next year's festival to walk home together again." Martha laughed softly, agreeing wholeheartedly. "I'd like that."

Continuing their stroll toward home, their steps felt lighter, their conversation warmer, both feeling quietly grateful for the festival that had brought them together. When they finally reached Martha's gate, James paused, tipping his hat again. "Goodnight, Martha. Thank you for the company." "Thank you, James," she replied warmly. "Until our next walk." She watched him walk slowly down the road, heart lifted by the gentle promise of friendship—and perhaps even more—that had blossomed beneath the stars on their long, lovely walk home.

Memory Prompts:

- Did you ever walk home from an event with a friend or sweetheart?
- Do you recall the feeling of walking at night in your town?
- What places felt safest to you growing up?

Conversation Starters:

- Do you enjoy walking for exercise or relaxation?
- Would you rather walk alone or with company?
- What's your favorite memory of a nighttime stroll?

The Old Love Song on the Jukebox

Carol and Joe slid into their usual booth at Daisy's Diner, the familiar scent of coffee and fresh-baked pie surrounding them like a warm hug. This diner had been their special place for decades, a quiet corner filled with simple pleasures and cherished memories.

As always, Joe reached into his pocket and pulled out a coin, sliding it across the table toward Carol. She smiled knowingly and stood, walking over to the vintage jukebox that stood proudly against the diner's wall. Carefully, she dropped in the coin, pressed a familiar set of buttons, and returned to their booth just as their favorite song filled the room.

It was the same tune they had listened to on their first date, so many years ago, right here at Daisy's. Joe had been so nervous then, tapping his foot anxiously under the table. Carol had smiled patiently, gently reassuring him until the song began to play and the tension melted away. They had shared milkshakes and whispered dreams of their future while the melody wrapped warmly around them.

Tonight, the song filled them again with that familiar warmth. Joe reached across the table, gently taking Carol's hand. His eyes sparkled softly, the music bringing a gentle smile to both their faces.

"Still my favorite," Carol said softly, glancing affectionately at Joe.

"Mine too," Joe replied, squeezing her hand gently. "Though it seems to get shorter every year."

Carol laughed warmly. "Or maybe we're just getting older."

They both chuckled softly, comfortable in the gentle truth of her words. Around them, the diner buzzed quietly—friends chatting, families enjoying dinner—but Joe and Carol felt as if they were in their own little world, created by the soft glow of neon lights and the comforting melody from the jukebox.

"Do you ever wish we could go back?" Joe asked thoughtfully. "Just for a moment?"

Carol considered quietly, then shook her head gently. “I love the memories, but I wouldn't trade today for anything.”

Joe smiled warmly, nodding in agreement. He understood what she meant; their life had changed through the years, but the love that began in this booth had only grown deeper and more precious.

When the song finally faded, they lingered quietly for a moment, savoring the gentle echo of its melody. Carol glanced at the jukebox again, its lights glowing softly, inviting them to stay a little longer.

“You know,” Carol said with a twinkle in her eye, “we could always play it again.”

Joe laughed softly. “Why not? We’ve got all night.”

Carol rose from the booth once more, smiling broadly as she returned to the jukebox. Soon, the familiar notes filled the diner again, drawing knowing smiles from the staff and a few regular customers who recognized the ritual.

Returning to Joe’s side, Carol slipped into her seat, sighing contentedly.

“You never tire of this?” Joe asked, already knowing the answer.

“Never,” she replied gently, reaching for his hand once again. And together, they sat quietly, hearts full, the jukebox serenading them sweetly into another evening at their favorite booth.

Memory Prompts:

- Did you have a favorite café or diner to visit?
- Do you remember a song that felt like “yours” with someone?
- Did you ever share a meal at a special place with friends or a partner?

Conversation Starters:

- Do you prefer live music or recorded songs?
- What’s your favorite tune to hear in public?
- If you could choose one song to play right now, what would it be?

The Keepsake Box

Sarah carefully lifted the small wooden box from the shelf, holding it gently in her hands. Its corners were worn smooth, polished by years of handling. Settling comfortably into her favorite chair, she slowly opened the lid, breathing in the familiar, comforting scent of cedar and nostalgia.

Inside, nestled together, lay tiny treasures collected over a lifetime: yellowed ticket stubs from theaters visited long ago, dried flowers pressed between the pages of old books, and small handwritten notes, ink now faded but still meaningful.

She reached first for a small seashell, recalling the beach vacation when her daughter Emily had excitedly discovered it. Sarah remembered Emily's bright laughter and sandy hands, proudly presenting her mother with this simple gift. She smiled softly, feeling the warm tug of memory.

Next, her fingertips touched a silk ribbon, frayed at the edges but still vibrant. It had once wrapped a bouquet given by her husband, Charles, on their anniversary. Sarah had saved it carefully, keeping it close to remind herself of the quiet strength and love that had filled their years together.

She shifted slightly, lifting another treasure: a tiny hand-painted stone with the word "Grandma" carefully lettered in childish script. Her granddaughter, Lily, had shyly handed it to her, eyes shining with pride. Sarah remembered the hug that followed, so warm and sincere, filling her heart with joy.

Each item she lifted from the box carried its own story. A feather found on a forest walk, an old photograph of friends, a button from her son's first coat—each preserved with quiet care, each tied to memories of people she cherished.

Sarah paused, holding one small note, written in Charles's steady hand. It simply said, "Thinking of you." She recalled how he would leave these notes tucked in unexpected places, tiny gestures that filled ordinary days with tenderness.

The box itself had been a gift, handmade by Charles, presented quietly one birthday long ago. “To hold our memories,” he’d said simply, his eyes warm with affection. And it had, becoming a quiet guardian of precious moments, each carefully saved and tucked away.

Sarah closed the box slowly, her heart full. She knew someday this box would pass to Emily, and then perhaps to Lily, each generation adding their own tokens of love and remembrance. For now, though, it was hers to treasure, a gentle reminder of a life richly lived, of love shared and joys preserved.

She returned the box to its shelf, content. Around her, the house felt peaceful, filled with echoes of laughter, whispers of past conversations, and quiet promises for the future.

Sarah knew she would return to her keepsake box many times, always finding comfort and joy in its familiar contents. Until then, she moved gently through the afternoon, thankful for the simple objects that could hold such powerful memories and quietly hoping her family would someday cherish these small reminders as deeply as she had.

Memory Prompts:

- Did you ever keep a box of mementos?
- What small object reminds you of someone you love?
- Do you recall a special gift that you’ve kept for years?

Conversation Starters:

- Do you enjoy keeping souvenirs from trips or events?
- What’s one item you’d never give away?
- If you could pass down one keepsake, what would it be?

Chapter 4: Friendship & Community

Friends and neighbors often make ordinary days feel special. They're the familiar faces we meet at the bus stop, the companions who brighten afternoons with cheerful conversation, and the helping hands always ready to lend support when it's needed most. This chapter celebrates those simple but powerful connections that turn neighborhoods into communities and acquaintances into lifelong friends. Maybe you remember someone who greeted you warmly each morning, or perhaps there was a knitting circle or gardening group where friendships blossomed easily. Community gatherings, such as lively potlucks, backyard games, or local parades, often brought joy through shared experiences and laughter. Even small gestures—neighbors chatting across fences, children delivering handwritten newsletters, or friends gathering around a table to play cards—can become cherished memories. As you read, you might recall a special person whose kindness made a difference, or an evening spent exchanging stories around a neighbor's kitchen table. Perhaps you'll remember watching your community come together for a celebration or quietly support one another through challenges. Whatever your memories, these stories will gently remind you of the warmth, laughter, and sense of belonging that friendship and community have brought into your life.

The Bench by the Bus Stop

Every morning, Leonard shuffled to the bench at the corner bus stop, a folded newspaper under his arm. For months, he sat alone, quietly watching cars pass and listening to the rhythm of neighborhood life. One day, Helen, a newcomer to the neighborhood, joined him on the bench, smiling gently as she sat down.

“Good morning,” she greeted, glancing at the headline of Leonard’s paper. “Anything interesting today?”

“Same news, different day,” Leonard replied, folding the paper onto his lap. “Though, I suppose that’s not always a bad thing.”

Helen chuckled softly. “True enough. My name’s Helen.”

“I’m Leonard,” he said, nodding politely. The bus arrived soon after, interrupting their conversation.

Each day afterward, the two sat together, waiting for the number 27 bus. Conversations began slowly, snippets about the weather or the local news. Gradually, they shared more—stories about family, favorite memories, and hobbies long abandoned.

Leonard discovered Helen had moved closer to her daughter after losing her husband, and Helen learned that Leonard used the morning bus ride to visit his favorite diner downtown, a comforting routine after retiring from his bookstore.

One particularly cold morning, Leonard didn’t show. Helen sat alone, shifting uneasily. She found herself watching anxiously, hoping he was alright. The following day, relief washed over her as Leonard appeared again, bundled warmly in a thick coat and scarf.

“I was worried yesterday,” she confessed quietly.

Leonard smiled, touched. “A slight cold,” he explained. “But I'm fine now, thanks for your concern.”

After that, the friendship blossomed into a comforting familiarity. Leonard would occasionally bring Helen a book he thought she'd enjoy, while Helen baked cookies that Leonard swore were the best he'd ever tasted.

Months later, during one warm spring morning, Leonard handed Helen an envelope. "Open it later," he said with a gentle smile.

Helen tucked it away, puzzled yet curious. When she opened it that afternoon, she found a handwritten note: "Thank you for making mornings brighter."

The next day, Helen arrived early, a small thermos of coffee in hand. As Leonard joined her, she poured two cups. "You know," she said softly, "I realized something yesterday. Waiting for the bus isn't really what keeps me coming back here."

Leonard raised his cup warmly, clinking it gently against hers. "Neither do I."

They sipped coffee in the quiet morning sun, cars rumbling by, and birds chirping softly. There, on that simple bench by the bus stop, two neighbors had discovered something wonderful—the quiet joy of companionship that transforms ordinary days into treasured moments.

Memory Prompts:

- Did you have a neighbor you often chatted with?
- Do you remember waiting for buses or rides in your youth?
- Who made you feel welcome in your neighborhood?

Conversation Starters:

- Do you prefer short chats or long talks with friends?
- What's your favorite way to pass the time while waiting?
- Would you enjoy a walk, a chat, or a cup of coffee with a friend?

The Knitting Circle

Every Tuesday afternoon, Eleanor opened her living room to four dear friends from the neighborhood. The women brought knitting needles and baskets full of colorful yarn, laughter and chatter filling the cozy space.

Eleanor’s small home, filled with faded family photographs and handmade quilts, became their sanctuary. There, surrounded by warmth, the friends knitted scarves and blankets while sharing stories, hopes, and everyday challenges. Over time, the stitches they wove formed a gentle fabric of friendship.

There was Doris, whose quick wit always sparked laughter. Mildred, quiet and thoughtful, knitted slowly and meticulously. June, a retired teacher, would guide them gently through complicated patterns, always patient, always encouraging. Then there was Rose, whose needles clicked briskly, her yarn seemingly dancing.

One rainy afternoon, Doris arrived holding a photograph. "Look what I found!" she announced with excitement. The women leaned closer. It was an old black-and-white picture of five young ladies at a community dance decades earlier, smiling broadly, arms around each other.

Eleanor’s eyes lit up. "Goodness! That was us! Remember those dresses?"

"Handmade, of course," Rose chimed in, laughing. "And look at those hairstyles!"

The group reminisced, the room glowing with memories. They recalled sewing circles, neighborhood dances, and afternoons spent on porches, each memory connecting them more tightly.

Weeks passed into months, their friendship deepening with every stitch. When Mildred lost her husband, her friends knitted quietly beside her as she mourned. They made meals, brought flowers, and filled her empty home with warmth. Mildred later said it was the quiet click of knitting needles in her darkest moments that reminded her she wasn't alone.

As winter approached, Eleanor suggested making something special. They agreed on a community project, knitting blankets and scarves for a local shelter. The women spent weeks working, their conversations filled with a sense of purpose. They carefully selected colors, patterns, and textures, knowing their small gift might brighten someone's life.

When the blankets were ready, June neatly folded each one, placing a small, handwritten note inside: "Knitted with warmth by your friends at the Tuesday knitting circle."

Together, they delivered their creations, feeling both pride and humility. Later, sipping tea at Eleanor's house, they reflected quietly on their work.

"You know," Doris said softly, "I never imagined knitting could mean so much."

Rose nodded thoughtfully. "It was never really about the knitting, was it?"

Eleanor smiled warmly, looking around at her dear friends. "It was always about us. Together."

They raised their cups, toasting the friendship woven gently through the rhythm of their afternoons. There, among skeins of yarn and unfinished projects, five friends found comfort, strength, and meaning. For them, every stitch was a gentle reminder of companionship, kindness, and the beautiful things that come from gathering around a simple circle of friends.

Memory Prompts:

- Did you ever take part in a club or group activity?
- Who taught you a craft or skill when you were younger?
- Do you remember a time when friends helped you through a challenge?

Conversation Starters:

- Do you enjoy making things with your hands?
- Would you rather knit, paint, or do puzzles with friends?
- What hobby would you like to learn today?

The Community Garden

At the end of Maple Street, behind an old wooden fence, neighbors gathered every Saturday morning. The small community garden brimmed with life, vegetables growing neatly in rows and flowers blooming cheerfully in shades of red, yellow, and lavender.

Arthur, who had spent decades working at the local hardware store, arrived early to open the gate. Soon after, Margaret appeared carrying trays of tomato seedlings, a floppy gardening hat shading her gentle face. Henry and Susan followed closely behind, their grandchildren eagerly scattering seeds into fresh soil.

As the sun rose higher, neighbors chatted while pulling weeds, watering plants, and pruning blossoms. Advice flowed freely alongside laughter, creating a welcoming atmosphere. Henry often joked about his carrots refusing to grow straight, and Susan playfully teased him about his "artistically challenged" produce.

Margaret, with her quiet voice, shared fond memories of her father's garden. "He taught me patience," she often said softly. "Watching those little sprouts always amazed me."

Over weeks, friendships took root. One afternoon, Arthur noticed Margaret quietly tending her tomato plants, a thoughtful expression on her face.

"Everything okay?" he asked gently.

"Oh, yes," Margaret smiled warmly. "Just thinking about my father. Gardening makes me feel closer to him."

Arthur nodded. "It's wonderful how some memories never fade."

Summer passed lazily, and soon the garden flourished. Vegetables grew heavy on vines, and bees buzzed happily around colorful blooms. Henry harvested his crooked carrots with pride, while Susan's grandchildren excitedly collected ripe strawberries. Margaret's tomatoes ripened generously, shared freely with neighbors.

When autumn arrived, the neighbors organized a harvest feast, setting tables in the garden's center decorated with fresh flowers. Each family prepared dishes from their crops: crisp salads, sweet corn, roasted vegetables. Margaret's tomato pie was the highlight, greeted by delighted sighs.

Arthur rose to speak. “It's amazing,” he said warmly, “how planting seeds has grown more than vegetables. It's grown friendships.”

Margaret's eyes glistened as Henry cheerfully toasted, “To crooked carrots and lasting friendships!”

Laughter filled the garden as neighbors lingered until sunset. Later, in the gentle dusk, Margaret and Arthur stood quietly among the plants.

“Thank you,” Margaret whispered, “for helping create this.”

Arthur smiled softly. “It's all of us, Margaret.”

Together, beneath a sky filling with stars, they understood the garden had nurtured more than plants—it had blossomed into a true community.

Memory Prompts:

- Did you ever grow your own vegetables or fruit?
- Do you remember the first plant you took care of?
- Who inspired you to love nature or gardening?

Conversation Starters:

- Would you prefer to grow flowers or vegetables?
- Do you like working outdoors or indoors?
- What's your favorite flower to see in bloom?

The Neighborhood Newspaper

When summer came to Willow Lane, five neighborhood kids gathered in Emily's backyard, determined to start their own newspaper. Emily, who loved writing stories, brought paper and markers. Jack, always full of ideas, promised he'd find exciting neighborhood news. Sam was the artist, ready to draw cartoons. And the twins, Lisa and Ben, volunteered to help deliver the finished product door-to-door.

In a shady spot beneath the large oak tree, the kids laid out their first edition on an old picnic table. They brainstormed enthusiastically, deciding to include stories about Mrs. Henderson's prized roses, Mr. Patterson's friendly Labrador named Rusty, and tips from Grandma Betsy about baking her famous blueberry muffins.

Emily carefully wrote out each story by hand, shaping letters with cheerful concentration. Next to her, Sam sketched Rusty chasing butterflies, while Lisa and Ben proudly wrote out headlines in colorful letters. Jack buzzed around, making sure every piece of news felt just right.

On Saturday morning, the friends went door-to-door, excitedly handing out copies of the "Willow Lane Weekly." At each house, neighbors smiled warmly, praising their hard work and creativity. Grandma Betsy laughed joyfully when she saw her recipe, promising to bake fresh muffins as a thank you.

Over the next weeks, the little paper became a beloved neighborhood tradition. Neighbors looked forward to seeing Emily's thoughtful articles and Sam's funny cartoons, often featuring Rusty's playful antics. The twins loved delivering the papers, feeling proud and important as they greeted neighbors by name.

One afternoon, as the children were assembling their latest edition, they noticed Mr. Patterson's usually cheerful face looking troubled as he walked down the street.

“Everything okay, Mr. Patterson?” Emily asked softly.

“Oh, Rusty’s wandered off again,” he replied, worry in his voice. “I’ve looked everywhere.”

Jack immediately spoke up. “Don’t worry, we’ll find him. And we’ll use the paper to help!”

Together, the friends hurriedly created flyers, drawing Rusty’s picture carefully and writing clear descriptions. Soon, the neighborhood rallied. Neighbors searched gardens and parks, calling Rusty’s name gently. By evening, Mrs. Henderson proudly appeared, Rusty happily trotting beside her. Everyone celebrated Rusty’s safe return with hugs and cheers, thanking the young newspaper team. Mr. Patterson was especially grateful, his eyes bright with relief.

“You’ve got a real newspaper here,” he said, smiling warmly. “You’ve made Willow Lane a true community.”

That Saturday, their paper featured Rusty’s adventure prominently, alongside heartfelt thanks to everyone who helped. The headline, written proudly by the twins, read: "Rusty Returns! Neighborhood Teamwork Saves the Day." Summer ended, but the Willow Lane Weekly lived on, a reminder of the friendship, kindness, and teamwork that connected them all. Though small and handmade, their neighborhood paper carried stories big enough to bring neighbors together.

And long after that first summer, Emily still smiled remembering those sunny days, when a few pieces of paper, some crayons, and good friends created something that meant so much more than news.

Memory Prompts:

- Did you ever make or read a neighborhood bulletin or paper?
- Do you recall writing stories or letters as a child?
- Did you ever work with friends on a shared project?

Conversation Starters:

- Do you prefer reading the newspaper or hearing the news on TV?
- What kind of stories do you enjoy most in the news?
- Would you enjoy helping children with a creative project today?

The Church Potluck

On the first Sunday of every month, neighbors gathered in the small church basement carrying dishes that filled tables from end to end. Warm aromas of fresh bread, roasted chicken, savory casseroles, and sweet pies mingled together, greeting everyone as they entered.

Mary, who had attended for years, always brought her beloved potato salad. She often whispered that the secret was fresh dill and a touch of mustard. Beside her sat Albert, known throughout town for his delicious apple pie sprinkled generously with cinnamon sugar.

Each potluck had its own rhythm of conversation and laughter. Children ran playfully, grabbing cookies when adults turned their backs. Older friends sat comfortably together, exchanging stories from potlucks past. New neighbors, always warmly welcomed, quickly became part of the community.

John, the pastor, moved through the room with a smile. He joked often that these meals nourished more than stomachs—they brought the neighborhood closer together.

One potluck afternoon, Mrs. Andrews, who recently moved to town, lingered nervously at the entrance, clutching a covered dish. Mary spotted her immediately. "Come sit here!" she called warmly. "What wonderful thing did you bring?"

Mrs. Andrews shyly lifted the cloth, revealing freshly baked biscuits, golden-brown and inviting. "Just biscuits," she murmured softly. "I hope they're alright."

Albert chuckled kindly. "Biscuits are never 'just biscuits' around here. Welcome to our table."

Mrs. Andrews relaxed, feeling more at home. The biscuits quickly vanished amid praise from all. When plates emptied and conversations quieted, John stood and gently raised his hands.

"I've realized something special about these potlucks," he began warmly. "It's not just about wonderful food. It's about how each one of us brings something special—like today's biscuits."

Smiles turned to Mrs. Andrews, who blushed with pleasure.

"Every dish, every person, makes this gathering meaningful," John concluded with a warm nod.

Mary leaned toward Mrs. Andrews with a gentle smile. "Your biscuits are already famous."

Laughter rippled warmly through the room, embracing all gathered. When evening came, neighbors packed leftovers, exchanged goodbyes, and invited each other to visit again soon.

Mary placed a gentle hand on Mrs. Andrews' shoulder. "I'm glad you came today."

"Me too," Mrs. Andrews replied softly. "I think I've found home again."

After that day, Mrs. Andrews' biscuits became a beloved potluck tradition, proof that even something simple, baked with kindness, could bring an entire community together.

Memory Prompts:

- Did you attend church or community dinners growing up?
- Do you remember a favorite dish always served?
- Who did you usually sit next to at these events?

Conversation Starters:

- Do you enjoy savory or sweet dishes more at gatherings?
- What's your favorite holiday meal?
- If you could share a meal with your community today, what would you bring?

The Neighborhood Parade

Every Fourth of July, the small neighborhood of Pine Street filled with music, laughter, and brightly decorated floats. Children waved flags, bicycles sparkled with streamers, and neighbors lined sidewalks, eager for the annual parade to begin.

At the heart of this lively procession was Joe Miller, the retired music teacher who proudly played trumpet in the community band. Each year, dressed in his crisp white shirt and bright red tie, Joe stood straight-backed and smiling, his trumpet gleaming in the summer sunlight.

Nearby, little Tommy Lewis, riding his tricycle wrapped in shiny ribbons, gazed admiringly at Joe. Tommy dreamed of joining the band one day, carrying a big drum or perhaps even playing the trumpet like Joe.

“Think I’ll ever play as good as you, Mr. Miller?” Tommy asked shyly.

Joe smiled warmly, kneeling beside him. “Of course, Tommy. Keep practicing, and one day we'll march together.”

As the parade began, Joe lifted his trumpet and led the band into a spirited march. Music filled the street, bright and joyful, echoing through windows and gardens. Neighbors clapped along, waving and cheering as familiar tunes drifted past.

Behind Joe, floats rolled gently along, carrying waving families, brightly dressed dancers, and happy children tossing candy. Laughter filled the air, mixing with music in a sweet melody of community spirit.

At the parade’s end, the neighbors gathered in the small park for refreshments, conversation, and games. Tommy, enjoying a bright red popsicle, watched Joe carefully polish his trumpet.

"How long did it take you to learn?" Tommy asked softly.

Joe chuckled kindly. "Longer than eating that popsicle. But every minute was worth it."

Tommy grinned, sticky-faced, nodding thoughtfully.

Summer turned to autumn, then winter. All through the seasons, Tommy practiced, determined to join Joe in the band someday. When the following July approached, Tommy proudly announced to Joe that he'd been practicing every day.

Joe smiled knowingly. "Well, Tommy, then I think you're ready to march."

On parade morning, Tommy stood nervously beside Joe, holding a small drum, his heart racing with excitement. As the band struck up the first notes, Tommy carefully beat the rhythm Joe had taught him. Together, they marched through the neighborhood, side by side, the young drummer and the seasoned trumpeter.

The neighbors smiled warmly as they passed, calling out encouragement and applauding loudly. Tommy felt pride rise inside him, knowing he was part of something special.

Later, resting under the shade of the park's old maple tree, Tommy looked up at Joe with shining eyes. "That was amazing, Mr. Miller!"

Joe gently patted Tommy's shoulder. "I told you, Tommy. Practice, patience, and community. That's what makes music—and life—wonderful."

Tommy nodded quietly, understanding Joe's words perfectly. Music had brought them together, and now Tommy knew what Joe had always known: that the true magic of the neighborhood parade wasn't in the music alone, but in the friendships formed along the way.

Memory Prompts:

- Did you ever watch or join a parade?
- Do you remember the sounds of drums or trumpets in the distance?
- Was there a holiday or event your town celebrated with music?

Conversation Starters:

- Do you prefer parades, fairs, or concerts?
- What's your favorite type of music to hear live?
- If you could ride on a float, what would it look like?

Helping Hands on Moving Day

Early one sunny Saturday morning, the Johnson family pulled into the driveway of their new home on Clover Street. Boxes piled high in their old station wagon, and a moving truck soon followed. It had been a long drive, and everyone was tired, feeling both excitement and a little uncertainty about starting fresh.

Before the Johnsons even had a chance to stretch their legs, neighbors began arriving. Carol, from next door, walked up smiling warmly, holding a tray of freshly baked muffins. Tom, who lived across the street, brought coffee and juice, introducing himself with an easy grin. Soon, more neighbors appeared with welcoming smiles, ready to help.

At first, Mr. Johnson politely protested, insisting they had everything under control. Carol gently shook her head, her voice warm and reassuring. "Around here, we always lend a hand. Besides, everything goes faster when friends pitch in."

Together, neighbors and family worked steadily. Boxes moved swiftly from truck to house, laughter echoing through rooms that had been silent for weeks. Tom joked good-naturedly about the weight of certain boxes, making even the heaviest tasks lighter. Carol carefully unpacked dishes in the kitchen, chatting easily with Mrs. Johnson about local schools, grocery stores, and her favorite places to visit around town.

As midday approached, the Johnson children, Sam and Lily, began feeling restless. Recognizing their energy, Tom invited them into his yard, where he set up a game of catch. Carol's granddaughter soon joined, and before long, the yard echoed with playful shouts and laughter.

By afternoon, furniture filled rooms, beds were assembled, and boxes neatly stacked. Feeling grateful, the Johnsons invited everyone to sit on the wide front porch. Carol poured cold lemonade, handing cups around as neighbors settled into comfortable conversation.

Mr. Johnson looked around, his expression one of sincere appreciation. "We can't thank you enough," he said quietly. "You've made today feel special. Like home."

Tom leaned back in his chair, smiling. "Well, that's what neighbors do, isn't it? We look out for one another."

Carol nodded warmly. "You'll soon find that Clover Street feels more like family than just neighbors."

Evening came gently, casting soft golden light over yards and rooftops. Neighbors slowly said their goodbyes, promising visits, invitations, and future cookouts. When everyone had gone, Mrs. Johnson looked out toward the quiet street, a soft smile on her face.

"You know," she said softly, "moving day was tiring, but this neighborhood already feels like home."

Mr. Johnson put his arm around her, watching their children laugh and chase each other happily in the yard. "I think you're right," he replied warmly. "We couldn't have found a better place to settle."

On Clover Street, the Johnsons quickly learned that a neighborhood was more than just houses and streets. It was friendly faces, helping hands, and open hearts—a community ready to welcome newcomers and make them feel they belonged. From that very first day, the Johnson family knew they had truly come home.

Memory Prompts:

- Did you ever move houses as a child?
- Do you remember neighbors helping your family?
- What made a new place feel like home to you?

Conversation Starters:

- Do you prefer city life or country life?
- What would your dream neighborhood look like?
- What's the kindest thing a neighbor has ever done for you?

Game Night at the Jones's

Every Friday evening, the Jones family opened their doors to neighbors and friends for game night. As dusk fell gently over Oak Lane, warm lights flickered through the curtains, and laughter drifted from open windows, drawing everyone inside.

Margaret Jones set out bowls of popcorn, plates of freshly baked cookies, and pitchers of lemonade. Her husband, Bill, carefully arranged board games across their large dining table, from old favorites like Scrabble and dominoes to colorful new ones the grandchildren adored.

As neighbors arrived, the room quickly filled with cheerful greetings and warm embraces. Friends chatted eagerly about the week's events, sharing stories, jokes, and news from around town. Soon, groups formed naturally around chosen games, each table buzzing with good-natured rivalry.

At one table sat Bill and his old friend Frank, engrossed in a lively game of checkers. Beside them, their wives Margaret and Anne laughed as they drew cards, each secretly confident she held the winning hand.

Across the room, younger neighbors teamed up for a spirited round of charades. Joyful shouts filled the air as teammates guessed wildly, applauding each clever or amusing effort. Even little Danny, barely six years old, proudly acted out clues that made the adults chuckle warmly.

As evening passed, neighbors switched games, welcoming newcomers with ease. When Margaret's fresh plate of cookies appeared, everyone paused happily to enjoy the treats, offering compliments that made her smile with quiet pride.

Then, amidst the relaxed chatter, Frank leaned back thoughtfully. "You know," he said, watching friends playfully argue over scoring rules, "it's funny how a simple game can make a night feel special."

Bill smiled warmly, nodding his agreement. "It's not really the games, though, is it? It's the people around the table."

Margaret squeezed Anne's hand affectionately. "Yes, it's about being together. It's about friendship."

The room quieted gently, each neighbor considering the truth of those words. After a thoughtful moment, Danny, unaware of the adults' reflection, cheerfully asked, "Who's ready for another game?"

Laughter burst forth again, joyful and bright. "Count me in!" Frank said eagerly, rubbing his hands together.

"Me too!" Anne added, grinning as she shuffled the cards.

Games resumed with new enthusiasm, neighbors eager to extend their evening just a little longer. As the clock approached bedtime, guests began to rise reluctantly, exchanging hugs and promises to meet again next Friday.

At the door, Frank paused, placing a gentle hand on Bill's shoulder. "These nights mean a lot, you know. Thanks for bringing us all together."

Bill smiled warmly, his eyes twinkling with contentment. "Margaret and I feel the same. Friday wouldn't be the same without you all."

As friends drifted home beneath the soft glow of streetlamps, laughter fading into peaceful quiet, everyone knew the Jones's game night had become more than just a weekly tradition. It was a cherished reminder of friendship, community, and the simple joy of being together.

Memory Prompts:

- Did you play card games or board games with family or neighbors?
- Do you remember a game you always won?
- Did you have a favorite game night snack?

Conversation Starters:

- Do you prefer board games, card games, or puzzles?
- What game would you like to play right now?
- Do you enjoy playing games more for fun or to win?

The Neighborhood Talent Show

Every summer, residents of Elm Street gathered eagerly at the community hall for the neighborhood talent show. It was a cherished tradition, bringing together young and old to share their unique skills, heartfelt songs, or simply to enjoy friendly laughter.

On the day of the show, Mrs. Bailey always arrived early to set out chairs and adjust curtains. She moved with practiced ease, humming gently to herself. Soon after, Charlie, a retired carpenter, arrived to help arrange the small wooden stage and hang festive decorations.

As neighbors began filling the hall, excitement filled the air. Children bounced in their seats, holding homemade signs to cheer their friends, while parents and grandparents settled comfortably, whispering anticipation.

The show began promptly at six, with little Emma stepping shyly onto the stage. Her voice quivered at first, but gentle applause quickly eased her nerves. Soon she was singing confidently, her sweet voice filling the hall and touching hearts.

Next came Bobby and Ted, brothers who performed a juggling act with tennis balls. Though they dropped more balls than they caught, their wide smiles and good-natured laughter made them instant favorites, drawing delighted cheers from the audience.

Midway through, Mr. Jenkins appeared on stage, wearing a colorful bowtie and carrying his accordion. He played lively folk tunes that had neighbors clapping joyfully along. Even quiet Mr. Thompson tapped his toes, his serious expression softened into a warm smile.

Then came the comedic highlight of the evening—Eleanor and Ruth, inseparable friends who performed humorous skits each year. Tonight they presented a playful routine about forgetful neighbors, cleverly incorporating jokes that gently poked fun at themselves and others. The hall echoed with laughter, deep and genuine.

When the laughter faded, young Sarah stepped forward. Soft-spoken and shy, she had never performed before. Holding a paper tightly in her small hands, she quietly began reading a poem she'd written about friendship and belonging. Her simple, heartfelt words captured the essence of their community, moving many listeners to tears.

As Sarah finished, silence lingered briefly before applause erupted, warm and sincere. Mrs. Bailey dabbed her eyes softly. Charlie rose to his feet, clapping vigorously. Around the room, neighbors smiled, realizing again what made these gatherings so special.

When the final performer left the stage, Mrs. Bailey addressed the audience warmly. "Tonight," she said gently, "we've shared music, laughter, and kindness. Most importantly, we've shared ourselves."

Later, as neighbors slowly headed home under starlit skies, everyone carried with them the evening's quiet joy. The talent show had reminded them of something they all treasured deeply: a community bound not only by shared streets but by warmth, laughter, and heartfelt connections.

Memory Prompts:

- Did you ever perform in front of others?
- Do you remember a family member with a special talent?
- Was there an event where your community came together to share skills?

Conversation Starters:

- Do you enjoy singing, storytelling, or listening?
- If you could learn a new skill, what would it be?
- What's your favorite performance you've ever seen live?

Neighbors at the Fence

Between the houses of the Harris and Anderson families stood a simple wooden fence, weathered gently by years of sunshine and rain. Though built to mark a boundary, this fence had become a place of gathering, laughter, and conversation.

Mornings often found Emma Harris watering her roses near the fence line, waving cheerfully when she saw Lucy Anderson stepping out with her cup of coffee. They'd pause to chat, sharing news about children, gardens, or plans for the day ahead.

"Did your tomatoes ripen yet?" Emma asked one sunny morning, carefully trimming blossoms.

Lucy smiled, nodding. "They did! I saved some for you. Let me grab them."

Emma laughed softly as Lucy hurried back, returning moments later with a small basket of bright red tomatoes. Passing them gently over the fence, Lucy whispered, "Careful—my tomatoes might not taste as sweet as yours."

Emma smiled warmly. "Anything grown by a friend tastes sweet enough."

Afternoons were livelier, especially when children returned home from school. The Harris twins, Ben and Molly, and young Josh Anderson often ran toward the fence, sharing stories, swapping toys, and comparing homework. Sometimes they played imaginative games, with the fence becoming a magical castle or pirate ship.

Evenings brought Mr. Harris and Mr. Anderson to the fence, their relaxed conversation carrying softly on warm breezes. They discussed work, sports, or plans for weekend barbecues, often ending with laughter and firm handshakes across the wooden boundary.

The families grew closer over the years, borrowing sugar, tools, or extra chairs for gatherings. They celebrated birthdays together, shared cookouts, and comforted each other during difficult times. When Mr.

Harris was recovering from surgery, the Andersons quietly delivered meals, placing dishes atop the fence with gentle notes of encouragement.

One summer afternoon, the neighbors gathered for an impromptu barbecue. Chairs were placed near the fence, plates of food handed easily across. Children laughed happily, while adults shared easy conversation, feeling more like family than mere neighbors.

Lucy glanced fondly at Emma, her voice gentle. "Funny how this fence never divided us—it always brought us closer."

Emma smiled warmly, nodding. "It was always more bridge than barrier."

Late that evening, when dishes were cleared and children tucked in bed, the two women lingered briefly by the fence. Stars twinkled gently overhead, crickets singing softly around them.

"You know," Lucy said quietly, "I'm grateful every day we ended up here, next to you."

Emma squeezed Lucy's hand warmly across the fence. "So am I."

Though a simple wooden fence stood between their homes, it never truly separated them. It had instead become a quiet meeting place, where neighbors turned into friends, conversations turned into connections, and simple kindness turned into lasting bonds of friendship.

Memory Prompts:

- Did you know your neighbors well when you were younger?
- Do you remember borrowing sugar, tools, or other things?
- Who was the kindest neighbor you ever had?

Conversation Starters:

- Do you prefer chatting across the fence or inviting friends inside?
- What makes a good neighbor to you?
- Would you rather live in a small town or a big city neighborhood?

Chapter 5: Everyday Humor

Laughter often shows up when we least expect it, in the simple mishaps and ordinary moments of daily life. This chapter is dedicated to those delightful surprises—the funny mix-ups, gentle misunderstandings, and small accidents that leave us smiling years later. Maybe you recall wearing a favorite hat that never seemed to sit quite right, or chasing after a shopping cart rolling away at the grocery store. Perhaps you've experienced the playful chaos of pets stealing food from tables or umbrellas turning inside out during a windy afternoon. Even something as small as a missing sock that becomes a family joke, or a beloved relative mixing up the words to a familiar song, can spark joy that lingers long afterward. As you read through these light-hearted stories, think back to your own humorous moments—the times when a lawn chair unexpectedly folded up, or someone grabbed the wrong coat after a gathering, or when a mischievous animal turned a quiet meal into an adventure. Everyday humor brightens our days, strengthens our bonds, and gently reminds us to never take ourselves too seriously. Sit back, enjoy, and let these cheerful stories bring a smile to your face and warmth to your heart.

The Crooked Hat

Charlie had been retired for years, but everyone in town still called him "Charlie the Postman." Even now, as he walked down Main Street each morning, people waved and called out to him like he still carried their letters and packages. And every morning, Charlie would smile and tip his old blue cap—the very same hat he wore for over thirty years of delivering mail. Only now, the hat never sat quite straight. It tilted to one side, making Charlie look just a little off-balance and a whole lot funny.

"Good morning, Charlie!" Mrs. Thompson would shout from her bakery door. "Your hat's crooked again!"

Charlie would adjust it, thanking her warmly, but two minutes later, it would slide right back to the side. At the barber shop, Joe would stop mid-cut, chuckling, "Charlie, that hat is gonna fall clean off one day!"

"Hasn't yet, Joe!" Charlie would answer, laughing as he gave it another useless push.

Neighbors tried everything. Mr. Harris suggested a paperclip inside the lining; it lasted half an hour. Lucy from the bookstore brought a sewing needle, carefully stitching the inside brim. It stayed straight until Charlie's first hearty laugh, then it tilted again, cheerfully refusing to be tamed.

At the café, friends placed bets—good-naturedly—on how many times Charlie would straighten his hat in one trip down the street. They'd laugh together, greeting Charlie each morning with warmth. And secretly, everyone loved that tilted hat, because it made him theirs. Charlie belonged to the town as surely as his hat belonged slightly sideways.

One sunny afternoon, Charlie sat on his front porch, chatting with his granddaughter, Emily. She tugged gently at the brim, giggling when it fell back.

"Grandpa," she asked, eyes twinkling, "why do you still wear this old hat anyway?"

Charlie leaned back, looking thoughtfully at the familiar blue fabric, faded from years in the sun and rain. "Well, Emily, every wrinkle, every tilt, every stitch—it's a memory. This hat has been through sunny days and storms, happiness and tears. When folks see it, they remember. It makes them smile. And you know what?"

Emily shook her head, smiling too.

"I like making people smile," Charlie said, eyes crinkling with pride. "So, I suppose, maybe the tilt is exactly the way it's supposed to be."

Emily laughed, nodding enthusiastically. From that day forward, Charlie stopped adjusting the hat. He wore it proudly, crooked and all. And the town continued to smile, loving their retired postman just as much as ever.

Memory Prompts:

- Did you ever own something you wore all the time?
- Do you remember a funny or unique piece of clothing you loved?
- Did a relative or friend have a trademark item they never left home without?

Conversation Starters:

- Do you prefer a favorite old hat or a brand-new one?
- What clothing item makes you feel happiest?
- If you designed your own hat, what would it look like?

The Runaway Grocery Cart

Frank never particularly liked grocery shopping. Still, he enjoyed greeting familiar faces and picking up freshly baked bread. Early one sunny morning, Frank pushed his slightly squeaky cart into Hill's Market, list in hand: bread, milk, apples, and coffee.

He strolled through the produce section, inspecting shiny apples and carefully filling a bag. When Frank spotted some perfectly ripe tomatoes nearby, he stepped away from his cart, forgetting how gently the store sloped.

With no warning, his cart quietly rolled forward. Frank turned just in time to see his groceries smoothly rolling away, picking up speed with every inch.

"Oh, goodness!" he exclaimed, dropping the tomatoes and hustling after the escaping cart.

Other shoppers smiled and pointed as the cart glided into the cereal aisle. Boxes of oatmeal and cornflakes seemed to lean aside as if to clear the way. Frank followed quickly, half embarrassed, half laughing, calling out, "Coming through!"

Mrs. Peterson, browsing cereals, stepped aside gracefully. "Looks like your cart's eager to check out without you, Frank!" she joked warmly.

Frank gave a sheepish grin. "I think it's making a break for freedom!"

By now, the entire aisle chuckled as Frank jogged after his runaway cart. It turned neatly toward the bakery counter, barely missing Mr. Hamilton, who was choosing muffins. "I think your groceries want dessert first!" he laughed, stepping back quickly.

At the bakery, Annie, who knew Frank's favorite bread, saw the cart heading her way and boldly stepped out from behind her counter. With a playful flourish, she halted its journey, smiling brightly at Frank.

"Thanks, Annie!" Frank puffed slightly as he finally caught up, his cheeks flushed but eyes twinkling. "This cart has a mind of its own!"

“I think it just missed me,” Annie teased, handing him his loaf of fresh sourdough. “Though I can’t promise it won’t run away again.”

Frank laughed along with Annie and everyone around him. His ordinary shopping trip had unexpectedly brightened everyone’s morning.

At checkout, Frank double-checked that his cart wasn’t escaping again, shaking his head with a grin. The cashier, Matt, teased gently, “I heard you had a bit of excitement today!”

Frank chuckled. “Just reminding everyone that shopping’s an adventure.”

On his way out, shoppers waved warmly, smiles still bright on their faces. Frank loaded his groceries into his car, carefully parking the cart in its place, giving it one last amused look.

From that day on, Frank’s weekly shopping trips felt lighter, and he realized that even chores could bring laughter—especially if the grocery cart decided to lead the way.

Memory Prompts:

- Did you ever have a funny shopping experience?
- Do you remember visiting markets or stores with family?
- Was there a favorite shop you liked going to?

Conversation Starters:

- Do you prefer shopping in small stores or big markets?
- What’s your favorite item to pick up when shopping?
- Do you enjoy browsing or making a quick list?

The Silly Umbrella Parade

Every spring, the residents of Maple Lane looked forward to their neighborhood parade. It wasn't a grand affair, but it was a cherished tradition, especially among the children. This year, the theme was umbrellas, and excitement buzzed through the street as kids and parents gathered in backyards and garages to decorate.

Billy and his sister Emma sat on the porch, carefully sticking glittery stickers and bright ribbons onto their umbrellas. Billy chose bold reds and blues, while Emma covered hers in delicate pink flowers and tiny bells that jingled softly as she moved. All around Maple Lane, umbrellas bloomed into joyful masterpieces of color.

Parade day arrived clear and sunny, perfect for a stroll through the neighborhood. Families gathered at the starting line near Mr. Carter's driveway. Parents snapped photos, and children proudly showed off their umbrella creations.

"Looks like we won't even need these today!" Billy laughed, holding his umbrella high.

Mrs. Reyes, the parade organizer, waved her arm enthusiastically, and the children began their cheerful procession. They walked slowly, twirling umbrellas overhead, waving at neighbors who clapped and called out encouragement. Emma's tiny bells chimed sweetly as she bounced along the sidewalk.

Halfway through the parade, a surprising gust of wind swept down Maple Lane. First, it gently lifted Billy's umbrella, flipping it inside out, ribbons streaming wildly. Emma shrieked delightedly as her umbrella did the same, its bells jangling loudly. Within moments, dozens of umbrellas inverted, their ribbons fluttering wildly, creating a bright spectacle of joyful chaos.

The children paused, looking at each other wide-eyed. Then, laughter erupted everywhere. Neighbors on their lawns clapped and chuckled at the delightful sight. Billy struggled to right his umbrella, but the breeze playfully kept turning it inside out again.

"It's the upside-down parade!" Mrs. Reyes called out happily, her own umbrella now resembling a brightly-colored bowl.

Children and parents joined in the laughter, continuing down Maple Lane with their now-upside-down umbrellas held high. Emma giggled, delighted by the silliness, bells ringing cheerfully with every step. Billy waved proudly to neighbors who applauded the unusual spectacle.

By the parade's end, Maple Lane had filled with warmth, laughter, and the shared joy of unexpected moments. Families lingered to chat, sharing stories about their rebellious umbrellas, while children traded ribbons and stickers, still giggling.

Years later, people on Maple Lane would fondly recall the parade when the umbrellas decided to take control. It wasn't the perfect march they'd planned, but everyone agreed—it had been the best parade yet.

Memory Prompts:

- Did you ever decorate objects for fun?
- Do you remember windy days from childhood?
- Did you ever join in playful group activities outside?

Conversation Starters:

- Would you rather decorate an umbrella, a hat, or a kite?
- Do you like bright colors or soft shades more?
- What's your favorite kind of playful group activity today?

The Sock on the Clothesline

In the cozy backyard of the Thompson home stood a wooden clothesline that stretched neatly from one end of the yard to the other. Every Saturday morning, Mrs. Thompson hung fresh laundry, letting it flutter gently in the sun and breeze, carrying the clean scent through the neighborhood.

One bright Saturday, after removing the dried clothes, Mrs. Thompson paused, puzzled. There, clipped firmly to the line, hung a single navy-blue sock. She didn't recognize it—it wasn't Mr. Thompson's, nor was it the boys'. Curious but busy, she shrugged and left it, certain someone would soon claim it.

Days went by, yet no family member admitted owning the sock. Soon it became a weekly curiosity, drawing playful attention from the Thompsons. Mr. Thompson joked it belonged to a secret visitor. The children speculated wildly, each theory sillier than the last: perhaps it belonged to a lost astronaut, a friendly ghost, or maybe even the neighbor's mischievous cat, Buttons.

As weeks passed, the lone sock remained stubbornly pinned to the line. It endured rainstorms, wind gusts, and even snow flurries, becoming part of the landscape. Neighbors took notice, chuckling quietly about the mysterious sock that had claimed permanent residency.

One afternoon, Grandma Thompson came by for a visit. She spotted the sock immediately. "Still no owner for that poor little sock?" she asked with amusement.

Mrs. Thompson smiled warmly. "Not yet. It's become part of the family, I suppose."

"Maybe it's bringing luck!" Grandma said, eyes twinkling. "You know, every household needs a bit of harmless mystery."

Soon enough, the sock had its own nickname: Lucky Blue. The children would salute it on their way to school, and neighbors playfully asked how

Lucky Blue was holding up. During barbecues or backyard games, friends joked about dressing it up for special occasions.

Then, one Sunday afternoon, during the annual neighborhood potluck, Mr. Hartley, who lived two doors down, paused suddenly as he balanced his plate filled with potato salad and barbecue chicken. Squinting carefully at the sock, he exclaimed with surprise, "I think that's mine!"

Everyone turned in amused silence. Mr. Hartley laughed sheepishly, explaining he'd lost the sock months ago while carrying a load from his dryer, and it must have blown across yards onto the Thompsons' clothesline. The yard erupted in laughter and applause, celebrating the sock's identity finally being solved.

"Well," Mr. Thompson said, pretending solemnity, "do you want it back, or has it become too famous?"

Mr. Hartley waved dismissively, grinning. "No, no, I think it's happier here."

Thus, Lucky Blue continued to hang proudly, a whimsical mascot that linked friends and neighbors, reminding everyone how humor could be found even in life's smallest mysteries.

Even years later, on sunny Saturdays, the Thompsons still smiled as they clipped their laundry to the line, the little navy sock swaying softly—still a charming reminder of laughter, friendship, and the day a simple sock became a neighborhood legend.

Memory Prompts:

- Did you ever hang laundry outdoors?
- Do you remember a family joke that lasted for years?
- Was there ever a household chore you enjoyed?

Conversation Starters:

- Do you prefer doing laundry or dishes?
- Have you ever lost a sock and never found it?
- Do you like fresh laundry scent or fresh bread smell more?

The Lawn Chair Collapse

On warm summer evenings, the Sullivan family always gathered in their backyard. Their favorite ritual involved settling into lawn chairs, sipping sweet iced tea, and sharing stories about their day as the sun gently set behind the oak trees. This evening was no different, except perhaps a bit warmer and a little more humid, perfect for relaxing outside.

As always, Mr. Sullivan took out his favorite old folding chair. It was faded, slightly frayed, and a little rusted at the hinges, but he insisted nothing was as comfortable. Despite gentle teasing from his family, he maintained that this chair was the best seat in the yard.

“Careful, Dad,” his daughter Laura joked, setting down a tray of lemonade. “One day, that chair might surprise you.”

Mr. Sullivan waved away her concerns. “Nonsense! This chair’s tougher than I am.”

With a confident grin, he eased himself backward, settling in with a satisfied sigh. But no sooner had he relaxed than a sudden snap echoed through the yard. The old chair gave way, gently collapsing and sending him sprawling backwards onto the soft grass.

The entire family froze for just a moment, then burst into roaring laughter. Even Mr. Sullivan, sprawled awkwardly, couldn’t help chuckling.

“I warned you!” Laura gasped, tears of laughter rolling down her cheeks.

Mr. Sullivan lay still for a moment, arms outstretched dramatically. “I think my pride is more damaged than my backside,” he confessed, laughing harder.

Mrs. Sullivan reached to help him up, unsuccessfully trying to suppress her giggles. “I suppose it was bound to happen eventually,” she said between chuckles, offering her hand.

Their young grandson Danny watched wide-eyed, then asked sincerely, “Grandpa, did the chair break because you’re old or because it’s old?”

Fresh laughter erupted again, filling the backyard. Mr. Sullivan, brushing grass from his shirt, smiled warmly at Danny. "Probably both, kiddo," he said, giving Danny a playful wink.

Neighbors, hearing the commotion, peeked over fences. Mrs. Moore from next door called out good-naturedly, "Everything all right over there, George?"

Mr. Sullivan raised a reassuring hand. "Just demonstrating the dangers of antique furniture!" he replied cheerfully, sparking yet another wave of amusement.

For the rest of the evening, the family reminisced about other funny incidents—the time Mr. Sullivan fell into the kiddie pool, or when their cat got tangled in the hammock. They shared stories until dusk turned into twilight, the incident becoming an instant family classic.

From then on, the broken lawn chair remained in the corner of the garage, too sentimental to discard. Every summer, at least once, someone playfully suggested Mr. Sullivan give it another chance. And every time, he'd grin, shake his head firmly, and settle into a sturdier chair, prompting new rounds of affectionate teasing.

Those warm nights taught the Sullivans something valuable: moments of unexpected laughter are often the ones you cherish most deeply—especially when the joke's lovingly on you.

Memory Prompts:

- Did you ever sit on a chair that broke unexpectedly?
- Do you remember family evenings outdoors?
- Did your family keep old furniture that held special memories?

Conversation Starters:

- Do you prefer sitting outside or inside to relax?
- What's the funniest accident you've seen at a family event?
- Do you enjoy telling funny mishap stories?

The Cat Who Stole the Sausage

On a sunny Saturday afternoon, Pine Street buzzed with excitement. It was the day of the annual neighborhood cookout, an event everyone anticipated eagerly. The smell of sizzling hamburgers, grilled vegetables, and spicy sausages filled the air, drawing friends and neighbors from their homes and into the festive street.

The star of the cookout was always Mr. Bailey, who proudly managed the grill, cheerfully greeting everyone who passed by. Wearing his favorite apron, he skillfully turned meats and veggies, sending mouthwatering aromas drifting through the neighborhood.

Nearby, children chased each other around picnic tables, adults chatted over iced drinks, and laughter echoed between yards. Among the crowd was a familiar local resident who wasn't officially invited but considered herself an honored guest—a curious little tabby cat named Ginger.

Ginger was known throughout the street for her clever mischief and daring escapades. Her antics had often caused friendly amusement, like the time she balanced delicately on Mrs. Cooper's fence, watching birds, or the day she squeezed through Mr. Grayson's porch railing and startled him out of an afternoon nap.

Today, Ginger sensed opportunity, her sharp green eyes locked on Mr. Bailey's grill. With feline precision, she approached silently, unnoticed by the chatting adults and playing children. Her nose twitched at the delicious scent of grilled sausages, and her tail flicked mischievously.

Suddenly, without warning, Ginger leapt gracefully onto the table beside the grill. Before anyone could react, she snatched a juicy sausage right off the hot grate with her mouth. The sausage dangled comically as Ginger paused, seemingly startled by her own boldness.

Mr. Bailey froze mid-flip of his spatula, eyes wide with surprise. "Hey! Ginger, that's not yours!" he exclaimed, half-amused and half-alarmed.

The neighbors turned, and a burst of laughter erupted as Ginger leapt from the table, the stolen sausage bouncing gently in her grip. She paused briefly in the middle of Pine Street, almost as if posing proudly, giving everyone a chance to admire her triumph.

Children clapped and pointed, delighted by the scene. Adults laughed warmly, shaking their heads. Ginger, sensing her mission accomplished, trotted confidently down the sidewalk, tail held high, sausage still swinging gently.

“Well,” Mrs. Cooper laughed, “I guess she’s earned it.”

Mr. Bailey chuckled, flipping another sausage onto the grill. “Maybe Ginger just wants to be part of the cookout tradition!”

Throughout the afternoon, the amusing incident became a favorite topic, with everyone sharing funny stories of pets from their past. Ginger became something of a neighborhood celebrity, forever known as the sausage-stealing cat of Pine Street.

From that day forward, each year at the cookout, Mr. Bailey jokingly grilled an extra sausage just for Ginger, setting it aside in a special dish. The neighbors would gather around, waiting to see if their favorite feline thief might make another surprise appearance. And Ginger, watching carefully from her favorite porch railing, never disappointed.

Memory Prompts:

- Did you have pets that ever stole food?
- Do you remember funny family pets from your past?
- Did animals often join your family gatherings?

Conversation Starters:

- Do you prefer cats, dogs, or other pets?
- What’s the funniest thing you’ve seen an animal do?
- Would you rather cook indoors or outdoors?

The Forgotten Song Lyrics

Every summer, the Campbell family held a gathering at Grandpa Joe's lakeside cabin. The tradition involved good food, lively storytelling, and, most importantly, their beloved evening sing-along around a crackling fire. Everyone eagerly anticipated Grandpa Joe's deep voice as he led them in familiar tunes, strumming his old guitar and encouraging everyone to join in.

This year was particularly special, as family members traveled from distant towns to join. Children roasted marshmallows, adults exchanged jokes, and laughter filled the air, mixing warmly with music from Grandpa's guitar.

After a lively rendition of "You Are My Sunshine," Aunt Clara requested Grandpa Joe's favorite classic: "Moon River." The family quieted, settling comfortably into blankets and chairs, waiting expectantly as Grandpa Joe cleared his throat.

He began confidently, his warm, gravelly voice filling the quiet evening. But as he reached the second verse, his expression suddenly shifted from confidence to confusion. His strumming slowed. His voice hesitated. "Moon River... wider than a... mile..." he sang, then paused, searching for words that eluded him.

Everyone leaned forward, supportive yet amused, waiting for the lyrics to return. Grandpa Joe glanced up sheepishly. "Well, folks, it appears the river just ran dry," he joked, triggering gentle laughter around the fire.

Unwilling to stop, he improvised, crafting new lines on the spot. "Moon River, don't know where it flows... can't remember how it goes...," he sang boldly, eyes twinkling mischievously. His spontaneous creativity drew giggles from the children and chuckles from the adults.

Encouraged by laughter, Grandpa Joe grew bolder, stringing together funny lines about moonlit frogs, lost boats, and friendly raccoons. The family clapped along, smiling brightly at each whimsical verse. Aunt Clara wiped away tears of laughter, declaring it the best version she'd ever heard.

When he finally reached the made-up finale, dramatically singing, "Moon River, hope I've sung enough... don't know the words, this song is tough!" everyone burst into heartfelt applause. Grandpa Joe stood, taking an exaggerated bow, his smile brighter than the firelight.

From that evening forward, Grandpa Joe's funny rendition of "Moon River" became the most requested song at family gatherings. The original lyrics were quickly forgotten, replaced by Grandpa's humorous verses. Each year, family members eagerly contributed their own lines, keeping the laughter fresh and the song happily evolving.

Even decades later, as younger generations joined, the tradition continued. The Campbell family never sang "Moon River" correctly again, nor did they wish to. Instead, it had become their playful family anthem, always a little different, always slightly ridiculous, and always reminding them how joy could emerge beautifully from a simple forgotten lyric.

Grandpa Joe's accidental improvisation had turned a musical mistake into a cherished memory, proving once more that laughter was the best tune of all.

Memory Prompts:

- Do you remember singing together with family or friends?
- Did you ever forget the words to a song or poem?
- What song always made you smile as a child?

Conversation Starters:

- Do you prefer singing or listening?
- What's a song you'd like to sing now?
- Do you enjoy music in the morning or at night?

The Wrong Birthday Gift Bag

Every year, the residents of Elm Street looked forward to Dorothy Miller's birthday party. Dorothy was beloved by neighbors young and old for her cheerful laugh and her legendary chocolate cake. This year's celebration was particularly special, as Dorothy was turning seventy-five. Friends gathered in her cozy backyard, decorating tables with colorful streamers and balloons that bobbed gently in the breeze.

Guests placed gift bags on a table beneath the apple tree, each labeled neatly with bright tags. Among the crowd, Mr. Peterson stood chatting with Mr. Andrews, holding his small gift bag proudly, though he'd forgotten to label it in his rush to arrive on time.

After cake and laughter, Dorothy sat down to open gifts. Surrounded by smiling faces, she reached for the first bag, a pretty lavender one without a name tag, assuming it was intended for her. Pulling aside the bright tissue paper, she peered inside, her eyes widening in surprise.

"Oh!" Dorothy exclaimed, laughing gently as she pulled out a small baseball cap featuring the local high school mascot. She placed it playfully on her head. "Well, this is unexpected!"

Confused murmurs and soft laughter spread among the guests. Mr. Peterson suddenly cleared his throat awkwardly. "Actually, Dorothy, I believe that one's for Tommy," he admitted sheepishly, pointing toward the young boy celebrating his birthday next door. Tommy stood by the fence, watching curiously through the pickets.

Dorothy broke into warm laughter, removing the cap and waving cheerfully to Tommy, who grinned brightly. "It suits you, Dorothy!" Tommy called back happily, prompting more laughter.

Red-faced but smiling, Mr. Peterson quickly handed Dorothy the correct bag, a lovely blue one with a ribbon. Dorothy opened it, revealing a delicate porcelain figurine. Everyone clapped appreciatively, but the humor had set a playful tone.

The laughter deepened further when Mrs. Carter, Dorothy's longtime friend, opened the next unlabeled bag, which turned out to contain gardening gloves obviously intended for Mr. Andrews. Holding them up, she jokingly modeled them, eliciting applause from her amused audience.

Soon, the gift-opening became a joyful puzzle. Guests cheerfully guessed owners of each unlabeled bag, causing playful chaos and waves of laughter. Dorothy held up a necktie clearly meant for Mr. Simmons, the postman, while Mrs. Thompson jokingly admired a pair of socks definitely intended for Mr. Reynolds.

Eventually, each misplaced gift found its way into the correct hands amid good-natured teasing and amused chuckles. Guests realized the mix-up had made the afternoon even more delightful.

When all was sorted out, Dorothy stood, eyes sparkling. "This is certainly one birthday we'll remember!" she said warmly. "Thank you all for your wonderful gifts, especially the surprises."

As neighbors hugged goodbye and walked home, laughter lingered in the air. The mix-up had turned Dorothy's birthday into a playful memory everyone treasured, reminding them that sometimes life's little mistakes created the happiest celebrations of all.

Memory Prompts:

- Did you ever receive the wrong gift by mistake?
- Do you remember exchanging gifts at gatherings?
- Was there ever a funny surprise you didn't expect?

Conversation Starters:

- Do you prefer practical gifts or sentimental ones?
- What's the most surprising gift you've ever given?
- Would you rather open a gift or watch someone else open one?

The Wrong Coat

Every November, the residents of Chestnut Lane came together for their annual autumn potluck dinner. Friends and neighbors eagerly prepared their best dishes, looking forward to good food, lively conversation, and warm company on chilly evenings. This year's gathering at the community center was as cheerful as always, filled with laughter, storytelling, and steaming casseroles passed around crowded tables.

As the evening ended, guests bundled up, retrieving their coats from the racks near the entrance. Among them was Mr. Tom Harrison, known for his quick smile but occasionally distracted mind. Without looking closely, Tom grabbed a dark wool coat from the rack, quickly pulling it on and heading home.

Only after arriving at his doorstep and reaching into his coat pocket for his keys did Tom realize something was wrong. Instead of keys, his hand touched a small paper bag. Confused, he pulled it out, discovering a small bundle of chocolate chip cookies neatly tied with a blue ribbon.

"Strange," he mumbled to himself, examining the coat carefully. It was similar to his, but upon closer inspection, clearly not the right one. Laughing softly at his mistake, Tom decided he'd return it in the morning and enjoyed one cookie before bed.

The next morning, Tom walked to the community center with the coat, greeted warmly by Mrs. Helen Jenkins, who had volunteered to tidy up after the potluck.

"Morning, Helen," Tom greeted, slightly embarrassed. "I took home the wrong coat last night. Any chance someone else might've noticed?"

Helen chuckled knowingly. "You're not the only one, Tom. We had quite a mix-up this year!"

Indeed, others had also mistakenly swapped coats, resulting in a playful morning reunion at the center, neighbors sheepishly exchanging garments, joking about becoming temporary caretakers of each other's belongings. Mr. Phillips laughed, handing back Mrs. Campbell's bright red coat. "I nearly wore this to church today!" he admitted, prompting laughter from the crowd. Meanwhile, Mr. Simmons cheerfully returned Mr. Reynolds's plaid scarf, jokingly confessing that it was too stylish for him. Each exchange prompted friendly teasing and amused laughter.

Finally, Tom held up the wool coat. "So, who baked these wonderful cookies?" he asked, smiling broadly.

From the back of the room, Mrs. Edwards raised her hand, eyes twinkling. "I wondered where those went! Thought I might've imagined packing them," she laughed. "Did you save any?"

Grinning sheepishly, Tom handed over the remaining cookies, apologizing playfully for eating one. "Couldn't resist. They were delicious."

Mrs. Edwards smiled warmly, passing cookies around to the neighbors, who eagerly accepted. The amusing coat confusion quickly turned into an impromptu morning gathering, bringing neighbors together once again.

From that day forward, the annual potluck included a humorous cautionary note: "Please double-check your coat before leaving—unless you'd prefer a morning reunion!" For years afterward, neighbors fondly recalled the humorous morning when swapped coats and misplaced cookies created laughter, warmth, and stronger friendships, all thanks to Tom's simple mistake.

Memory Prompts:

- Did you ever mix up your belongings with someone else's?
- Do you remember a coat or jacket you loved wearing?
- Did you ever find something funny in a pocket?

Conversation Starters:

- Do you prefer long coats or short jackets?
- What's the most unusual thing you've found in your pocket or bag?
- Do you enjoy hand-me-downs or prefer new clothes?

The Unruly Choir of Frogs

In the gentle twilight of a warm June evening, neighbors from around Willow Pond gathered for their annual lakeside picnic. Blankets spread across the grassy banks, picnic baskets opened to reveal homemade sandwiches, salads, and pies, and friendly chatter mingled with the calm sounds of nature.

Every year, after everyone had eaten and dusk began to settle softly over the water, the community enjoyed a tradition: singing favorite old songs under the open sky. Mr. Thompson usually played his guitar, Mrs. Ramirez brought out her violin, and young Ellie Baxter led everyone in cheerful renditions of familiar melodies.

This particular evening, however, nature seemed eager to join the festivities. As Ellie started singing a sweet tune, a single, deep croak echoed from somewhere near the pond's edge. A few neighbors chuckled lightly, enjoying the funny interruption.

But as Ellie continued bravely, more croaks quickly joined the first. Soon, an entire chorus of frogs began serenading the neighborhood, growing louder and more enthusiastic, drowning out the guitar and violin altogether.

Ellie paused mid-note, blinking in surprise. Mr. Thompson stopped strumming, raising an eyebrow toward the pond. The frogs, unaware or unconcerned about their disruption, croaked merrily onward, as if determined to become the evening's headline act.

A ripple of amused laughter ran through the gathered neighbors. Mrs. Ramirez jokingly bowed toward the pond, saying, "Well, clearly we have some new stars this year!"

Young Billy Porter jumped up excitedly. "Let's sing along with them!" he shouted gleefully, encouraging the others.

Smiling at the delightful absurdity, Ellie nodded brightly, waving her arms as if directing a real choir. Neighbors began croaking playfully, imitating their amphibious accompanists. Soon, laughter filled the air as everyone joined the unruly choir, creating a humorous harmony that echoed cheerfully across Willow Pond.

Even shy Mr. Carver joined in, holding his deep croak extra-long, eliciting applause and joyful giggles from the children. The frogs, perhaps startled by their unexpected backup singers, momentarily quieted, leaving the neighbors to croak loudly on their own, drawing more laughter.

Finally, after several joyful minutes, the frogs resumed their symphony, now seemingly coordinating their croaks perfectly with the playful human voices. The neighborhood choir and its new frog members shared an unforgettable duet, their combined music echoing gently into the night.

As darkness fully embraced Willow Pond, neighbors packed up their picnic baskets, waving goodbye with lingering smiles. Their annual gathering had become something more delightful than they ever imagined, thanks to a group of small, unexpected performers.

Years later, neighbors still laughed fondly about the night the frogs of Willow Pond formed their own choir, teaching everyone that the best gatherings often came with spontaneous humor and unexpected guests. And each summer evening afterward, families paused to listen, always smiling when the frogs began their familiar, joyful chorus.

Memory Prompts:

- Did you ever hear frogs or crickets on warm nights?
- Do you remember times when nature made everyone laugh?
- Did your family enjoy outdoor evenings together?

Conversation Starters:

- Do you prefer the sounds of birds or frogs in the evening?
- What natural sound do you find most relaxing?
- If you could visit a peaceful place in nature today, where would it be?

Help Others Find Their Story

As you journey through these pages, you might have found yourself smiling at familiar moments—a joyful childhood memory, a shared laugh, or a comforting reminder of simpler times.

But did you know your honest opinion about this book could spark those same feelings for someone else? By leaving a brief, genuine review on Amazon, you help guide readers who are seeking comfort, laughter, or nostalgia.

Your feedback—positive, negative, or somewhere in between—is deeply valued. It costs nothing and takes less than a minute, yet your words can profoundly influence another reader's day.

This isn't just about reviewing a book; it's about connecting through stories that matter, creating a quiet community built on shared experiences. Your voice might inspire someone new to discover these gentle moments of joy and reflection.

Would you join me in spreading that kindness?

Thank you so much for your thoughtful contribution.

Scan to leave a review on Amazon

Chapter 6: Pets & Animal Companions

Animals have a special way of finding their way into our hearts and becoming beloved family members. They're the companions who fill our days with playful antics, comfort us with quiet affection, and bring gentle humor into our routines. This chapter shares stories that celebrate these lovable creatures, from puppies stumbling adorably through their first steps to curious cats that curl up in the most unexpected places. Perhaps you remember a dog who welcomed every guest with eager friendliness, or a mischievous kitten who delighted in hiding your belongings. Maybe a simple goldfish once surprised you with its lively personality, or you shared laughter over an adventurous pet who found ways to brighten your everyday moments. As you read, take a moment to recall your own animal friends, their quirks, and the happiness they brought into your life. Whether it was a cat perched patiently at the window, a dog loyally fetching the morning newspaper, or a cheerful bird singing sweetly at dawn, these companions taught us kindness, patience, and unconditional love. Allow these heartwarming stories to gently remind you of the furry, feathered, or finned friends who enriched your days and filled your home with warmth and joy.

The Puppy with Big Paws

Oliver was only ten weeks old, but his paws were enormous. They looked like they belonged to a dog twice his size, and wherever he walked, those oversized paws led the way—often in unpredictable directions. At first, the Wilson family wondered if their new puppy would ever learn how to walk without stumbling, but it wasn't long before his playful clumsiness became their favorite entertainment.

Oliver's big paws tripped him when he chased balls, making him somersault awkwardly into the grass. When he dashed across the kitchen tiles, his paws slid out like a cartoon character, sending him skidding and spinning. The Wilson children laughed until tears rolled down their cheeks, and even their parents couldn't resist smiling at his antics.

Grandpa Ed, however, sat quietly in his favorite armchair during Oliver's playful escapades, watching with mild amusement. He was reserved by nature, and since his wife passed, he'd grown even quieter. The family hoped Oliver might bring Grandpa Ed a bit of cheer, but the puppy seemed almost intimidated by the older man's silence.

One afternoon, Oliver was chasing his favorite rubber duck around the living room. He misjudged his step and tumbled head over tail, landing directly at Grandpa Ed's feet. The family held their breath, watching as Grandpa Ed slowly leaned forward. Oliver froze, looking up with wide eyes and his tongue hanging sideways.

"You've got paws bigger than my work boots, son," Grandpa Ed said gently, reaching down and picking up Oliver. The puppy relaxed immediately, his tail wagging so hard his whole body wiggled. The old man chuckled—a sound the Wilsons hadn't heard in a long time—and Oliver gave his face an enthusiastic lick.

From then on, Oliver sought out Grandpa Ed every chance he got. If Grandpa Ed went out to the porch, Oliver was right there, stumbling over his paws to sit at his feet. In the evenings, when Grandpa Ed read his newspaper, Oliver would curl up nearby, occasionally falling asleep with his oversized paws sprawled out, twitching gently in his dreams.

One day, Grandpa Ed took Oliver to the park. They moved slowly down the walking path, Oliver constantly bumping into Grandpa Ed's legs with his clumsy steps. Yet the older man never minded. When neighbors stopped to greet them, Grandpa Ed proudly introduced Oliver, highlighting the puppy's massive paws as if they were trophies.

"Look at these paws," he'd say, laughing. "You'd think he was part bear!"

At home, the family saw Grandpa Ed smiling more often. Oliver had somehow found the one person in the house who needed him the most, and in his awkward, joyful way, he gave the older man a reason to laugh again.

As months passed, Oliver eventually grew into his paws. He was no longer the clumsy puppy but a gentle dog who always stayed near Grandpa Ed's side. But even when Oliver was fully grown, Grandpa Ed would pat his head lovingly and chuckle.

"You may have grown into those paws," he would say warmly, "but you'll always be my clumsy puppy."

Memory Prompts:

- Did you ever have a pet when you were young?
- Do you remember the first time you held a puppy or kitten?
- Was there an animal that made you smile every day?

Conversation Starters:

- Do you prefer dogs, cats, or another pet?
- What's a funny thing you've seen a pet do?
- If you could have any pet now, which would you choose?

The Cat in the Knitting Basket

Every afternoon, Carol settled into her favorite chair by the living-room window, placing her knitting basket carefully at her feet. It held bundles of yarn in all her favorite colors: lavender, sky blue, rose pink, and buttery yellow. These were the shades that reminded Carol of spring mornings in her mother's garden.

One particular afternoon, just as Carol had selected the perfect shade of blue, she heard a gentle rustling from the basket. Peering down, she discovered a pair of bright green eyes blinking mischievously back at her. It was Lily, the family's curious young tabby cat, comfortably curled up atop Carol's yarn collection.

"Now how did you get in there?" Carol laughed, gently lifting Lily out of the basket. But as soon as Carol turned back to her needles, Lily snuck right back in, pawing at a ball of lavender yarn and unraveling it across the floor. Carol sighed, pretending to scold her, but the playful mischief made her smile.

From then on, Lily made the knitting basket her favorite spot. No matter how carefully Carol placed the basket or covered it with a cloth, Lily found her way in, rolling around joyfully and tangling every strand. Soon, Carol's knitting sessions turned into playful battles, gently retrieving yarn from Lily's playful grasp.

One evening, Carol's grandchildren, Anna and Jake, came for dinner. They burst into giggles when they spotted Lily, half-hidden in a colorful nest of yarn.

"She looks like a princess in a rainbow castle!" Anna exclaimed, her eyes wide with delight.

Jake laughed and reached for Lily, but the mischievous cat darted away, pulling a stream of yarn behind her. Carol and the children chased Lily through the living room, under tables, and around chairs, laughing until their sides hurt. By the time they caught Lily, the entire room was decorated in cheerful tangles of yarn.

Looking at the colorful mess, Carol simply shook her head, smiling warmly. The knitting basket had become more than just a place to hold yarn; it was now the center of joyful chaos that brought everyone together.

Days later, Carol decided to knit Lily something special—a small blanket of her own. As Carol worked, Lily watched intently from the basket, purring loudly. When Carol finished, she placed the soft blanket inside the basket, hoping Lily would finally leave her yarn alone.

But the playful cat had other ideas. Instead of lying neatly on her new blanket, Lily proudly carried it around the house, dragging it onto sofas and under beds. It was clear she preferred yarn adventures to resting quietly.

Eventually, Carol accepted that the knitting basket would always belong to Lily, no matter how tangled the yarn became. Instead of frustration, she felt warmth and joy, knowing Lily's antics had transformed simple afternoons into treasured memories filled with laughter.

Now, whenever friends visited and saw Lily curled contentedly amid the colorful strands, Carol would shrug playfully and say, "Who knew a little cat and a basket of yarn could create such a happy mess?"

Everyone laughed, knowing that sometimes the sweetest memories come from the most delightful tangles.

Memory Prompts:

- Did you know someone who loved knitting or sewing at home?
- Do you remember a pet sneaking into funny places?
- What hobby did you enjoy sharing with family or friends?

Conversation Starters:

- Do you prefer cats that are playful or calm?
- What color yarn or fabric do you like best?
- Would you enjoy watching someone knit or sew today?

The Dog Who Loved Mail Carriers

Max wasn't your ordinary dog. He had shiny black fur, soft floppy ears, and eyes that sparkled whenever someone came down the street. Unlike other dogs in the neighborhood, Max didn't bark at strangers. Instead, he welcomed everyone, especially mail carriers, with an eager wag of his tail and a playful dance.

The mail carrier who came down Willow Lane each morning was named Susan. She had worked the same route for years and knew every mailbox by heart. Yet, no mailbox made her smile like the Wilson family's—because that meant seeing Max.

Every morning, as Susan turned onto Willow Lane, Max was already watching from the porch window. The moment he spotted her, he bounded down the steps, his tail spinning like a helicopter blade. Susan always laughed and reached into her pocket for a small treat she brought especially for him.

"Good morning, Max," she'd say warmly, scratching him behind the ears. Max responded by offering his paw, then rolling onto his back for a quick belly rub. The neighbors would often pause to watch this daily greeting, smiling at the unusual friendship that brightened the street.

One day, Max was particularly excited. It was raining lightly, and Susan had her big yellow raincoat and wide-brimmed hat on. Max found this fascinating. As Susan approached, he danced in circles, playfully jumping toward her hat. Surprised, Susan laughed and held the hat out, letting Max gently grasp it in his mouth. He pranced proudly around the yard, showing off to the neighbors who had gathered to see what all the commotion was about.

The following morning, Max waited eagerly for Susan, but someone new walked up the sidewalk. It was a young man named Tom, looking nervous as he carried a heavy mailbag. Max tilted his head, confused, but soon rushed forward with his usual friendliness.

Tom froze when he saw the energetic dog coming toward him, but instead of barking, Max nudged Tom's hand gently with his nose. Relaxing, Tom knelt down and smiled.

"You must be Max," Tom said softly. "Susan told me about you."

That afternoon, Susan stopped by without her uniform. She explained she was retiring and wanted to say goodbye properly. Max whined softly, sensing the change, and sat quietly by her side. Susan hugged him tightly, promising to visit often.

In the weeks that followed, Tom became a welcome part of Willow Lane, thanks to Max's enthusiastic greeting each morning. Tom began carrying treats in his pocket, just as Susan had done. The neighbors watched with fond smiles as Max continued his joyful ritual, helping Tom feel right at home.

One evening, Susan came back for a visit, and Max recognized her immediately. He ran straight into her arms, nearly knocking her over with happiness. She laughed and hugged him close.

"It's good to see you too, buddy," Susan said warmly, glancing around at the neighbors gathered nearby. "I missed this."

Everyone agreed. It was Max, with his playful spirit and unconditional friendship, who had turned simple mail deliveries into cherished moments shared by all on Willow Lane.

Memory Prompts:

- Did your pets get excited when visitors came?
- Do you remember a kind neighbor or delivery person?
- Did you ever train a pet to do tricks?

Conversation Starters:

- Do you prefer morning or afternoon walks with a pet?
- What's your favorite animal to watch outside?
- Would you rather have a playful or calm pet?

The Goldfish with Personality

When Eleanor received a small goldfish as a birthday gift, she didn't expect it to have much of a personality. It was just a tiny, orange fish swimming circles in a simple glass bowl. Yet, from the moment Eleanor placed the bowl on her kitchen table, she noticed something special.

The fish seemed to watch her as she prepared tea each morning. Its round eyes followed her hands as she moved around, placing sugar cubes into her cup or spreading jam on toast. Eleanor found herself talking to the little fish, explaining the news headlines or her plans for the day. Soon, she named him Bubbles, after the gentle sound he made nibbling at the water's surface.

One day, Eleanor invited her friend Margaret over for afternoon tea. As they chatted, Margaret pointed at Bubbles with a surprised laugh.

"Eleanor, your goldfish is watching us," Margaret said, amused.

Eleanor nodded, smiling. "Oh yes, he does that all the time. Watch this."

She gently tapped her finger against the glass, moving it slowly across the bowl. Bubbles eagerly followed, his tiny fins fluttering rapidly. Margaret was astonished.

"It's almost as if he's playing with you!" she exclaimed.

From that day forward, Bubbles became famous in Eleanor's circle of friends. Everyone wanted to see the goldfish who behaved like a playful puppy. Visitors often brought treats, and one neighbor even gifted Eleanor a larger tank, complete with colorful pebbles and plants for Bubbles to explore.

Bubbles took happily to his new home. He swam excitedly around the plants, investigating every corner. Eleanor even added a miniature castle decoration, and Bubbles quickly claimed it as his private spot, peeking out whenever someone approached.

One afternoon, Eleanor's granddaughter, Lucy, came for a visit. Lucy was feeling a bit shy at first, but Bubbles quickly drew her attention.

"Grandma, your fish looks friendly," Lucy said softly.

"Why don't you introduce yourself?" Eleanor suggested with a gentle smile.

Lucy leaned close and whispered, "Hi, Bubbles."

To her amazement, the goldfish darted toward her voice, his tiny mouth opening and closing as if greeting her. Lucy giggled, delighted, and spent the rest of her visit playing with Bubbles. She tapped the glass gently, leading the cheerful fish in playful loops around the tank.

From that moment, Lucy visited more often, each time bringing drawings she made of her aquatic friend. Eleanor hung these colorful pictures around the kitchen, proud that her little goldfish had brought them closer.

Eventually, everyone in Eleanor's life came to adore Bubbles. Friends joked that he must be a genius, but Eleanor simply smiled and said, "He's just a small fish with a big heart."

Over time, Eleanor realized that it wasn't just Bubbles who had transformed her days. It was the laughter and warmth he brought into her home. He showed her—and everyone who met him—that sometimes the smallest creatures could bring the greatest joy.

Each evening, before bed, Eleanor would whisper goodnight to her tiny companion. And every night, Bubbles would flick his tail, sending small, cheerful splashes as if whispering goodnight in return.

Memory Prompts:

1. Did you ever keep fish or watch them swim in ponds?
2. Do you remember giving names to your pets?
3. Was there an animal you cared for that had a big personality?

Conversation Starters:

1. Do you enjoy aquariums or zoos more?
2. What name would you give a pet fish today?
3. Do you find water or gardens more relaxing?

The Cat Who Rode the Bus

In the quiet little town of Maplewood, everyone knew the number eight bus that circled the neighborhood each morning. It stopped by the bakery, the library, and the local park, carrying friendly faces and pleasant conversations from one end of town to the other. But recently, the bus had a new and rather unusual passenger.

Mittens, a plump gray cat with white paws, had discovered the joy of bus travel. It all started one crisp autumn morning when the bus doors hissed open at the corner stop. Mittens had been sitting nearby, grooming her whiskers. Curious about the open door and the gentle hum inside, she stepped onto the bus without hesitation.

"Well, hello there," said Frank, the bus driver, surprised but amused. He watched Mittens casually stroll down the aisle, settling gracefully into an empty seat near Mrs. Collins, who visited the library daily.

Mrs. Collins chuckled softly. "Looks like we've got company."

Mittens purred contentedly as the bus moved along, completely at ease among the other passengers. When the bus circled back and reached her stop again, Mittens hopped down, stretching lazily before trotting home.

At first, everyone thought it was a one-time adventure. But the next morning, Mittens was waiting patiently at the same stop. When Frank opened the door, she stepped aboard as though she'd done it her entire life. Within days, Mittens was considered a regular rider on the number eight.

People began looking forward to seeing her. Children giggled excitedly, and neighbors shared smiles whenever she chose their seat. The cat even seemed to have favorite spots: Mrs. Collins was her morning companion, while Mr. Reynolds from the hardware store was Mittens' preferred afternoon partner.

Word spread quickly around Maplewood. Visitors sometimes rode the bus just to see Mittens, laughing as she sat serenely, gazing out the window or batting playfully at loose threads on passengers' sweaters.

One particularly cold morning, a new rider named Sarah stepped onto the bus. She had recently moved into town and wasn't quite feeling at home yet. As Sarah sat alone, Mittens softly jumped onto the seat beside her, gently nudging Sarah's hand with her head. Sarah smiled for the first time in days.

"It's like she knew I needed a friend," Sarah told Frank later.

Soon, Mittens wasn't just riding the bus—she was connecting people. Passengers began chatting more often, swapping stories about their furry traveling companion. Even shy neighbors found it easier to strike up conversations, always beginning with, "Did Mittens sit with you today?"

Eventually, a small sign appeared at the bus stop featuring Mittens' picture and a simple phrase: "Home of Maplewood's Most Famous Passenger." It made everyone smile, proud that their little town had a cat clever enough to ride a bus all on her own.

Through Mittens' quiet charm and casual adventures, the people of Maplewood rediscovered the simple joys of companionship and unexpected friendship. And each morning, as Frank opened the bus door, he'd greet his furry passenger warmly, "All aboard, Mittens!"

The gentle cat would climb aboard with her usual grace, purring softly as if she knew exactly how important her presence had become.

Memory Prompts:

- Did you know an animal that liked to wander around town?
- Do you remember a surprising place where you saw a pet?
- Did you ever take the bus or train regularly?

Conversation Starters:

- Do you prefer traveling with company or alone?
- Would you enjoy seeing a pet on public transport?
- What's your favorite memory of local travel?

The Dog and the Newspaper

Every morning, like clockwork, Archie the golden retriever eagerly waited at the front door, his tail wagging and his eyes sparkling with anticipation. Archie had one important job in the Miller household: fetching the daily newspaper. It was a task he took seriously, even if the result wasn’t always perfect.

The routine started when the sun was barely up, with Archie sitting at the window, his ears perked up, waiting for the familiar sound of Mr. Brown's old delivery truck rumbling down the street. The moment the newspaper landed softly on the lawn, Archie bounded outside in a cheerful blur of golden fur.

Archie had plenty of enthusiasm, but he lacked gentleness. He often grabbed the paper with a bit too much excitement, shaking it playfully, causing pages to scatter like oversized leaves around the yard. The first few times, Mrs. Miller laughed as she gathered up the damp and crumpled pages, grateful for Archie's good intentions.

As days passed, Archie improved slightly, managing to bring the newspaper to the porch, though it often arrived somewhat soggy from his enthusiastic grip. No matter the condition of the paper, the Millers always praised him warmly, patting his head and calling him their "good boy."

One rainy morning, Archie dashed out as usual, his paws splashing joyfully through puddles as he grabbed the newspaper. When he returned, the paper was soaked completely through. He dropped it at Mr. Miller's feet with a proud look, water dripping onto the porch floor.

Mr. Miller chuckled and gently scratched Archie's ears. "A little extra damp today, Archie, but you still got it!"

From that day on, Archie seemed determined to keep the paper as dry as possible. He tried new tactics, including dragging it carefully under the porch roof before picking it up, or occasionally balancing it delicately between his front teeth. Some days were better than others, but the family never minded. The entertainment Archie provided each morning was far more valuable than reading crisp headlines.

One day, the Millers' granddaughter Emily stayed overnight. Early the next morning, Emily stood quietly at the window, watching Archie’s daily adventure unfold. She laughed loudly as he carried the paper in slow motion, concentrating carefully to avoid causing damage. When Archie finally placed it gently at the front step, Emily clapped excitedly.

“You did it, Archie!” she cheered, throwing her arms around his neck.

Archie wagged his tail happily, sensing he'd finally perfected his morning task. Yet, the next day, he was back to his playful antics, tossing the paper joyfully into the air and leaving a trail of pages across the lawn.

Neighbors soon grew accustomed to the humorous scene, waving to the Millers as they walked by and joking about Archie's delivery skills. They even began calling him the neighborhood "paper dog," affectionately celebrating his imperfect but heartfelt efforts.

As the years passed, Archie continued his special delivery, never losing his joyful spirit or playful approach. And every morning, as he proudly dropped the soggy paper at their feet, the Millers smiled warmly, grateful not only for the day's news but for Archie’s loving dedication and the endless laughter he brought into their lives.

Memory Prompts:

- Did you or your family ever have a helpful pet?
- Do you remember reading the paper with loved ones?
- Was there a pet that surprised you with its cleverness?

Conversation Starters:

- Do you prefer reading the news in print or hearing it?
- What’s your favorite part of the morning routine?
- If a pet could bring you anything, what would you want it to be?

The Cat at the Window

Bella was a sleek, tuxedo-colored cat with bright amber eyes that missed nothing. From her favorite spot on the windowsill, she carefully observed every movement outside. The Parker family often joked that Bella was the neighborhood's quiet watchdog, even though she never left the safety of her indoor perch.

From her window, Bella saw everything. Each morning, birds landed softly on the fence, singing cheerfully. Bella would crouch down, ears perked, whiskers twitching. She was always ready, as if planning a daring adventure she would never actually take.

Then there was Mr. Thompson's dachshund, Scrappy, whose yappy walks drew Bella's attention like clockwork. She would sit straight, eyes following every jump and playful spin of the tiny dog. The Parkers chuckled at her intensity, imagining she was supervising Scrappy's noisy routine.

On Wednesdays, the garbage truck rumbled by loudly, making Bella leap off her perch in surprise, only to return moments later with a disdainful stare. Her family laughed softly, interpreting her look: "Who invited them to interrupt my morning?"

One afternoon, Bella's attention was captured by two squirrels racing around the oak tree. She pressed her paws against the glass, chirping softly. The Parkers watched, amused by her excitement and determination to reach the squirrels through the invisible barrier.

"She still hasn't figured out that glass," Mr. Parker remarked.

Mrs. Parker smiled warmly. "But she'll never stop trying."

Soon neighbors became accustomed to Bella's daily vigil, waving as they passed by. Bella rarely responded—until the day little Emma from next door paused to wave enthusiastically. "Hi, kitty!" Emma called out brightly.

To everyone's surprise, Bella placed her paw gently against the window, returning Emma's greeting. Emma giggled, thrilled to have made a new friend. After that, the two regularly exchanged silent waves through the glass.

Bella's window-watching quickly became a charming routine for the Parkers, offering them gentle moments of laughter and reflection. Visitors soon began checking the window upon arrival, curious to see what had captured Bella's interest that day. Friends joked she was the family's unofficial greeter.

One quiet evening, as the Parkers relaxed after dinner, Mrs. Parker glanced affectionately at Bella, who was gazing thoughtfully at the fading sunset.

"Funny how one small cat can make a home feel complete," she remarked softly.

Mr. Parker nodded warmly. "She reminds us every day to slow down and enjoy life's simple moments."

Unaware of her growing fan club, Bella continued her dedicated watch over Maple Street. To her, the window was simply a magical place filled with endless adventures. And to everyone else, Bella's silent observations were joyful reminders of the happiness found in the little things.

Memory Prompts:

- Did you ever have a pet that loved to sit by the window?
- Do you remember a favorite view from your childhood home?
- Did animals ever make you laugh with their antics?

Conversation Starters:

- Do you enjoy birdwatching or stargazing more?
- If you had a pet's view for a day, what would you like to watch?
- Do you prefer quiet pets or playful ones?

The Dog Who Stole the Blanket

On chilly evenings, nothing pleased Henry more than settling into his favorite chair with a warm blanket and a good book. But lately, Henry had to be careful about one thing: his dog, Toby. Toby, a friendly, shaggy mutt with eyes that sparkled mischievously, had discovered the joy of stealing Henry's blanket.

It always started innocently enough. Henry would sit down, wrapping himself comfortably in his thick, plaid blanket. Moments later, Toby would wander over, tail wagging gently. He'd sit quietly at Henry's feet, looking up with big, innocent eyes.

"You have your own bed," Henry would gently remind him, pointing to Toby's soft cushion in the corner.

But Toby had other plans. Slowly, he'd edge closer, placing his chin softly on Henry's knee, offering the sweetest look he could muster. Henry, unable to resist, would scratch behind Toby's ears affectionately, returning to his reading.

That was Toby's moment. With one swift move, the playful dog would grab a corner of the blanket in his teeth and tug it gently away, wagging his tail in delight.

"Hey!" Henry would laugh, gripping the blanket. "That's mine!"

But Toby never gave up easily. Soon, their playful tug-of-war had both of them laughing. Occasionally, Toby won, dashing away triumphantly with the blanket trailing behind him, Henry pretending to grumble while secretly smiling at his dog's antics.

One evening, Henry's granddaughter Sophie came to visit. After dinner, she sat on the sofa reading, wrapped cozily in the familiar plaid blanket. Toby noticed immediately and trotted over, ears perked and tail swishing with excitement.

"Watch out, Sophie," Henry warned with a chuckle. "He's sneaky."

Before she could ask why, Toby gently grabbed the blanket's edge and pulled, eyes twinkling playfully. Sophie laughed, holding tight, turning their game into a cheerful wrestling match.

"You're a thief, Toby!" Sophie giggled, finally giving in and allowing him to win.

Proudly, Toby dragged his prize to the carpet, curled up on top, and sighed contentedly, looking as pleased as if he'd captured buried treasure.

Sophie smiled warmly. "Maybe he just wants to feel included."

Henry nodded, watching Toby settle happily. "I think you're right. He always likes being near."

After that night, Henry began placing a second, smaller blanket beside his chair. Toby quickly claimed it, dragging it close whenever Henry sat down to read. They each had their own, yet Toby still occasionally made playful attempts to steal Henry's. The tradition became a warm routine they both enjoyed. Soon, family and friends began to look forward to watching their playful tug-of-war. It was a simple, joyful sight that brightened everyone's evening, bringing smiles and laughter each time.

One quiet night, Henry gently stroked Toby's fur as the dog snoozed nearby, wrapped snugly in his own blanket. Henry smiled softly, grateful for his companion's playful spirit and warmth. He knew that even on the coldest nights, Toby's mischievous ways kept their home filled with laughter and comfort. "Steal as many blankets as you like, buddy," Henry whispered fondly. "You've already stolen my heart."

Memory Prompts:

- Did your pets ever try to sleep on your bed or chair?
- Do you remember a pet that liked to curl up close?
- Did you have a blanket or pillow that was special to you?

Conversation Starters:

- Do you prefer a warm blanket or a warm fire?
- Do you enjoy sitting with pets while reading or watching TV?
- What's your favorite cozy spot at home?

The Mischievous Goat

When the Dawson family visited Uncle George's farm each summer, the children eagerly anticipated seeing the animals. There were gentle cows, chatty chickens, and horses grazing quietly in the field, but the star attraction was always Charlie, the farm's mischievous goat.

Charlie was small, lively, and endlessly curious. Uncle George often joked, "Watch your hats and jackets—Charlie loves borrowing things without asking!"

The family quickly realized how true this was. On their first morning, laughter filled the air as Aunt Mary chased Charlie across the yard, trying to retrieve her flowered apron that dangled from his mouth.

"Charlie!" she called, laughing as the goat playfully jumped away.

Later that day, while the children played catch, Charlie quietly approached the fence, gently pulling Emma's bright red sweater free and running off, proud of his prize. Emma giggled, chasing after him. Charlie eventually dropped the sweater, only to begin nibbling on Daniel's shoelaces instead.

Throughout their visit, Charlie remained true to his playful reputation. Laundry disappeared from the clothesline, gardening gloves mysteriously moved locations, and the screen door was often nudged open by Charlie's curious nose. Each playful episode ended with laughter, as the family lovingly retrieved their belongings.

One evening around a cozy bonfire, the Dawsons happily recalled Charlie's amusing pranks.

"I never imagined doing farm chores could be this entertaining," Aunt Mary said, shaking her head and smiling.

Uncle George chuckled. "Life would be dull without Charlie around."

As if hearing his name, Charlie suddenly appeared, quietly nibbling on Uncle George's straw hat.

"Oh, not again!" Uncle George exclaimed, laughing good-naturedly as he gently retrieved his hat and scratched Charlie affectionately.

By the end of their stay, everyone had a favorite Charlie story to share. Each playful incident had transformed simple moments into unforgettable memories.

When it was time to leave, Charlie stood near the car, watching curiously as they loaded their bags. The children waved goodbye, promising they'd visit again soon. Charlie bleated cheerfully, as if already planning his next prank.

Driving away, Emma sighed fondly. "I'll miss Charlie the most."

"Me too," Daniel agreed. "Next time, I'll bring extra shoelaces."

Their laughter echoed in the car, leaving Uncle George and Aunt Mary smiling warmly from the porch. Charlie stood proudly beside them, happily chewing a forgotten handkerchief—completely unaware he'd become the family's favorite memory from their farm adventures.

Memory Prompts:

- Did you ever visit relatives with farm animals?
- Do you remember feeding chickens, cows, or goats?
- What farm visits stand out in your memory?

Conversation Starters:

- Do you prefer visiting farms, parks, or gardens?
- Have you ever milked a cow or fed farm animals?
- What's your favorite farm animal?

The Puppy in the Picnic Basket

It was a perfect spring day, and the Parker family had decided to have a picnic by the lake. They packed sandwiches, fruit, and freshly baked cookies in their wicker picnic basket, along with a cozy blanket to spread on the grass. Everyone was excited—especially their playful new puppy, Daisy.

Daisy was a fluffy spaniel with a mischievous nature and boundless energy. From the moment the Parkers started preparing the picnic, Daisy bounced around their feet, wagging her tail eagerly, clearly sensing the excitement.

"Be careful," Mr. Parker warned, laughing as Daisy nearly tripped him. "At this rate, we might forget something important."

When everything was finally packed and ready, Mrs. Parker closed the lid of the basket firmly, unaware that Daisy had her own plans. As soon as everyone turned their backs to gather hats and jackets, Daisy saw her chance. Quietly, she nosed open the lid, hopped inside, and curled up among the food, tail wagging.

"Has anyone seen Daisy?" Emma asked, looking around.

"She's probably chasing butterflies again," Mr. Parker replied, smiling.

Arriving at the lakeside park, the Parkers chose a sunny spot near the water. Mr. Parker carried the heavy picnic basket, wondering why it seemed heavier than usual.

"Maybe I packed too much food," Mrs. Parker joked, as they unfolded their blanket beneath the trees.

As soon as Mr. Parker placed the basket on the grass and opened the lid, out popped Daisy, grinning broadly and wagging her tail enthusiastically. Everyone jumped back in surprise, then burst into laughter at the sight of their cheerful puppy surrounded by sandwiches and cookies.

"Oh, Daisy!" Emma laughed, picking up the mischievous puppy. "What were you doing in there?"

Daisy barked happily, pleased with the attention. The family gently unpacked the basket, grateful the food had survived Daisy's surprise appearance mostly intact, except for a slightly squished sandwich and a few missing cookies.

Settling down, the Parkers enjoyed their meal, sharing bites with Daisy, who seemed especially proud of herself. Emma and her brother, Ben, tossed a ball around, with Daisy eagerly chasing after it, returning with grass-covered paws and a happy expression.

As the afternoon passed, other families nearby stopped to admire Daisy, laughing warmly when the Parkers shared the story of her surprise appearance from the picnic basket. Daisy quickly became a local celebrity, basking happily in all the attention and extra pats on her fluffy head.

When it was time to head home, Daisy hopped right back into the basket, hoping for another ride. This time, everyone noticed immediately.

"No more surprises today, Daisy," Mr. Parker said affectionately, lifting her out and carrying her in his arms.

Driving home, Emma gently stroked Daisy's soft fur. "This was the best picnic ever," she said softly. "Yes," Mrs. Parker agreed warmly. "Thanks to our little stowaway."

From then on, every family picnic included an extra basket just for Daisy. Though she never again jumped in with the food, the Parkers always smiled, remembering the playful puppy who had once turned a simple family picnic into a delightful adventure.

Memory Prompts:

- Did you ever have a pet that loved hiding in funny places?
- Do you remember a family day outdoors with animals around?
- Did you ever get surprised by something in a bag or box?

Conversation Starters:

- Would you rather bring a pet to a picnic or leave it at home?
- What animal makes you smile the most?
- Do you enjoy quiet picnics or lively ones?

Chapter 7:
Seasons & Celebrations

Each season brings its own special rhythm, inviting us to slow down, gather together, and enjoy traditions that tie generations together. Whether planting fresh pansies to welcome spring or watching fireworks on a warm July evening, these moments create joyful memories we carry through life. This chapter celebrates the comfort found in familiar routines and festive gatherings, like autumn fairs with pies baking and laughter echoing through the air, or quiet winter nights spent singing carols with neighbors at the doorstep. Maybe your memories include carefully decorating hats for an Easter parade, raking leaves only to joyfully scatter them again, or gathering with loved ones around a Thanksgiving table full of familiar dishes. Perhaps you remember the excitement of a family reunion, with everyone adding their signature to a handmade quilt, or a simple summer lemonade stand run by children in the neighborhood. As you read these stories, allow yourself to recall your favorite seasonal traditions and festive celebrations. Remember the tastes, sights, and sounds that made each occasion special, and let these narratives gently lead you back to those joyful moments when the simplest gatherings became lasting treasures.

Springtime Window Boxes

As winter's grip loosened and warmth slowly returned to our little neighborhood, I always knew exactly when spring had arrived. It wasn't simply marked by the calendar or birds singing; it was the day my grandmother announced it was finally time to fill the window boxes.

That morning, the sun would always seem brighter, a little softer perhaps, carrying with it a fresh, earthy scent that filled me with anticipation. Grandma would rise early, heading to the garden center down the street while I eagerly awaited her return. Soon she'd appear at our gate, carrying trays brimming with pansies—cheerful faces of yellow, purple, and vibrant pink peering out at the world.

"Springtime has arrived," she'd say proudly, smiling as she set the flowers down gently on our front steps.

We'd lay out everything we needed, arranging pots, bags of fresh soil, and watering cans side by side along the porch. Grandma wore gardening gloves, but I loved the cool dirt against my palms, the way it slipped softly through my fingers, leaving earthy traces beneath my nails. Carefully, Grandma demonstrated how to lift each pansy from its pot, gently loosening the roots before nestling it into its new home. I copied her movements, clumsy at first, but soon falling into rhythm, feeling as though each plant and I had become friends. Grandma hummed softly, occasionally whispering encouragement as we worked.

"Do flowers really listen, Grandma?" I asked one day, amused by her gentle whispers.

"Oh, absolutely," she answered earnestly. "They bloom brighter if they feel wanted."

After all the flowers were planted, we stepped back together to admire our work. The vibrant petals nodded in the breeze, their colors instantly transforming the plain windows into bursts of cheerful life. Throughout the coming days, I'd rush home from school, running straight to the windows, my heart lifting every time I saw a new flower had bloomed. Neighbors passing by would often pause, commenting on how our little house seemed to announce the arrival of spring to the entire street.

On afternoons when the air felt especially sweet, Grandma and I would sit outside, sipping lemonade and watching butterflies flit gracefully between blossoms. She would tell me stories of her own childhood gardens, filled with flowers I'd never heard of, colors even more vivid than ours, and fragrances that made you dream. Her memories became part of the planting, as essential as sunlight or rain.

One evening, Grandma found me sitting quietly by the open window, lost in thought as twilight turned everything golden.

“What’s on your mind, dear?” she asked softly.

I sighed contentedly. “I’m just happy. It feels good to see flowers again after such a long winter.”

She nodded gently. “That’s why we plant them every year. Flowers remind us that brighter days always follow the cold ones.”

As the days lengthened, the pansies flourished, spilling over the edges of the boxes in colorful cascades. They became more than just decoration—they were symbols of hope, of renewal. Each spring, long after Grandma was gone and I planted flowers in window boxes of my own, I could hear her voice whispering softly, telling me how every flower deserved encouragement, reminding me how warmth and love could coax something beautiful from even the smallest seed.

Memory Prompts:

- Do you remember planting flowers in spring?
- What was your favorite springtime scent?
- Did you ever decorate windows or porches with plants?

Conversation Starters:

- Do you prefer spring flowers or autumn leaves?
- What’s your favorite flower to see after winter?
- Do you enjoy gardening alone or with company?

Fourth of July Lanterns

When I was a child, Independence Day meant fireworks and picnics, but for me and my cousins, it was all about lanterns. Every Fourth of July, as dusk settled, our family would gather in Grandma's backyard. Blankets covered the grass, lemonade pitchers were filled, and picnic baskets overflowed with sandwiches, chips, and Grandma's famous apple pie.

Yet, the main event wasn't the food or even the fireworks. It was the colorful paper lanterns we spent all afternoon preparing. We'd sit together at picnic tables, busy with crayons, markers, scissors, and glue, decorating each lantern uniquely. Mine always featured stars and stripes, carefully drawn and shaded with meticulous attention, while my cousin Lily preferred flowers and cheerful patterns. Grandpa would help us tie strings, explaining patiently, "These will hold the lanterns steady so they don't float too far away."

As darkness began to fall, excitement rippled through us like electricity. Grandma lit tiny candles placed carefully inside each lantern, illuminating our artwork from within. I still remember the gentle glow of candlelight on her face, smiling softly as she handed me mine.

Holding tightly to our strings, we lined up on the grass, hearts pounding with anticipation. Grandpa counted down loudly, dramatically: "Three...two...one...release!"

Our lanterns lifted gently into the sky, floating upward like small glowing balloons. I remember tilting my head back, watching in awe as they danced and bobbed gently through the twilight, each a tiny glowing heart against the darkening sky. Lily would cheer, clapping her hands, eyes sparkling. Even the adults seemed captivated, standing together quietly, murmuring softly at the beauty above.

At some point, distant fireworks began bursting into colorful explosions on the horizon, but none of us paid much attention. Our lanterns were quieter, softer, almost magical in their slow, graceful ascent. Sometimes, a lantern drifted slightly away, and we'd watch it anxiously, silently willing it to float safely. Occasionally, neighbors spotted our glowing creations and waved from their own backyards, adding to our excitement.

One year, as we watched our lanterns climb into the night, Grandpa softly told us stories of his own childhood celebrations—how he and his friends lit sparklers, drawing bright circles of light in the dark. Grandma smiled quietly, listening beside him, content in the shared warmth of family memories. Their stories became as precious as the lanterns themselves, creating a bond that made those nights unforgettable.

When the lanterns finally vanished into the night sky, leaving only memories and whispered hopes behind, Grandma always sighed happily and said, "Just like wishes, carried up to the stars."

Years later, even after Grandma and Grandpa passed and cousins scattered to distant places, I still find myself outside on the Fourth of July, gazing upward. In my imagination, the lanterns still drift quietly among the fireworks, lighting up the night in their own gentle way. Each lantern represented more than just childhood fun; they were quiet reminders that sometimes simple moments, shared together, glow brighter and linger longer than the loudest celebrations.

Memory Prompts:

- Did you celebrate Independence Day or similar holidays?
- Do you remember the first fireworks you saw?
- What celebrations brought your neighborhood together?

Conversation Starters:

- Do you prefer fireworks, music, or parades on holidays?
- What colors do you like most in a firework show?
- Would you enjoy sparklers or lanterns more?

The Harvest Festival Pie Contest

Every autumn, when the leaves turned gold and red, our village prepared for the annual Harvest Festival. It was a tradition that everyone eagerly anticipated, but no event drew as much attention as the pie-baking contest. From early in the morning, the sweet aroma of baking fruit filled every kitchen, drifting warmly through windows into the crisp fall air.

My mother was famous for her apple pie, known to have a perfectly flaky crust and just the right balance of cinnamon and sugar. Each year she'd rise at dawn, quietly slicing apples with expert precision as I sat sleepily at the table, mesmerized by the swift movements of her hands. I can still picture her apron dusted with flour, cheeks flushed from the warmth of the oven, her smile brightening our cozy kitchen.

At the festival, tables lined the main street, filled with pies of every imaginable variety: pumpkin, pecan, blueberry, and cherry. Village bakers eyed one another's creations playfully, engaging in friendly banter as they placed their entries carefully, hoping to impress the judges. Nearby, children ran laughing between stalls filled with crafts and fresh produce, their laughter mingling with the cheerful music drifting through the town square.

This particular year, Mrs. Harper, our elderly neighbor known more for her flower gardens than baking skills, surprised everyone by placing her pie proudly beside my mother's. Hers looked humble compared to the elaborate lattice and golden crusts of other contestants, but she stood beaming, hands folded calmly before her apron.

As the judges made their rounds, tasting small bites and nodding thoughtfully, the suspense grew. Families crowded around, holding their breath as the judges finally stepped forward to announce their decision.

"Third place," the head judge proclaimed, "goes to...Anna Bennett's blueberry delight!" Claps echoed warmly as Anna blushed happily.

"Second place, Sarah Miller's apple pie," he continued, and my mother gave a graceful nod, receiving cheers from friends nearby.

"And first place," he paused dramatically, eyes twinkling, "goes to...Mrs. Harper's sweet pear and honey pie!"

Surprise swept through the crowd, quickly followed by delighted applause. Mrs. Harper's eyes widened in disbelief as neighbors warmly patted her back and congratulated her, praising her courage to join the contest for the first time. My mother approached, smiling genuinely as she hugged Mrs. Harper tightly. "I'm so proud of you," she whispered. "You deserved to win."

Mrs. Harper chuckled softly, her voice trembling slightly with emotion. "To be honest, I thought I'd mixed up the sugar and salt," she admitted shyly, making everyone laugh heartily.

That evening, as neighbors gathered around the bonfire with slices of pie in hand, there was more laughter than ever. My mother nudged me gently, her eyes glowing with happiness as she whispered, "You see, sometimes life gives us sweet surprises when we least expect it."

Years later, whenever autumn colors paint the trees, I find myself smiling at the memory of Mrs. Harper's unexpected victory, reminded warmly of how joy can arrive in the simplest moments—and the most delicious pies.

Memory Prompts:

- Did your town host fall festivals or markets?
- Do you remember helping gather fruits or vegetables?
- Was there a time you or someone you knew entered a contest?

Conversation Starters:

- Do you prefer apple pie or pumpkin pie?
- What's your favorite fall flavor?
- Would you enjoy visiting a harvest market today?

The Easter Bonnet Parade

In our small town, Easter Sunday was never complete without the annual Easter Bonnet Parade. The event transformed our usually quiet streets into lively gatherings, filled with laughter, music, and an impressive assortment of brightly decorated hats. Children, adults, even pets joined in, each proudly showing off bonnets lovingly created at kitchen tables in the days leading up to the parade.

I remember clearly one particular Easter, when I was eight years old. My mother had suggested we decorate our hats together, turning our dining room table into a festive workshop. She carefully placed ribbons, flowers, feathers, and beads in colorful heaps, smiling warmly as I surveyed the options in awe.

"What if mine isn't as pretty as the others?" I asked, suddenly shy as I stared at the empty white hat in front of me.

Mom smiled reassuringly. "The most important thing is that your hat makes you happy," she said gently, handing me a bright blue ribbon. "Let's make something you'll love to wear."

Together, we wrapped ribbons around the brim, attached clusters of silk daisies, and sprinkled tiny, glittering beads along the edges. I remember feeling proud and excited, glancing at my reflection in the hallway mirror, amazed at our creation.

Easter morning arrived with sunshine, casting a gentle warmth over the town. Families lined up along Main Street, dressed in their Sunday best, hats proudly displayed atop carefully styled hair. My heart fluttered nervously as I took my place among the other children. Each hat seemed more creative than the last—there were hats decorated with colorful paper butterflies, tiny birds nestled among twigs, and even miniature Easter eggs balanced carefully on springs.

As the parade began, a cheerful marching band played, their melodies setting the joyful pace. Spectators clapped and waved, and I soon forgot my worries, caught up in the excitement of the moment. Looking around, I noticed smiles everywhere, as everyone admired the creativity and effort each hat represented. Even Mr. Thompson's dog had a small bonnet tied beneath his chin, wagging his tail proudly at the delighted laughter he inspired.

Near the end of the parade route, a gust of wind suddenly swept through, threatening our delicate hats. Children giggled and held tightly to their creations, and adults laughed good-naturedly as they hurriedly adjusted theirs. A feather from Mrs. Johnson's elaborate bonnet danced away into the sky, prompting gentle laughter from the crowd.

By the parade's end, we all gathered at the community center, sharing lemonade and cookies. Friends and neighbors admired each other's hats, exchanging compliments and cheerful banter. I remember my mother gently squeezing my shoulder, whispering proudly, "Your hat was wonderful, the very best you've ever made."

That Easter Bonnet Parade taught me something I've carried through my life: the joy of creating something beautiful isn't about competing or impressing others. Instead, it's about sharing laughter, creativity, and warmth with those around us. Even now, when I see bonnets displayed in shop windows around Easter, I remember the happiness of that sunny day, warmed by the simple joy of creating together.

Memory Prompts:

- Did you ever decorate or wear a special hat for a holiday?
- Do you remember attending spring celebrations?
- Did you enjoy egg hunts or other Easter traditions?

Conversation Starters:

- Do you prefer spring parades or autumn fairs?
- What holiday tradition would you like to try again?
- Do you enjoy decorating with flowers or lights more?

Autumn Leaves in the Basket

Every autumn, as the days grew shorter and the air became crisp, my brother Sam and I eagerly awaited the moment when the leaves changed from their summer green into brilliant shades of gold, crimson, and burnt orange. For us, the annual leaf-collecting competition had become a cherished tradition—one we approached with as much enthusiasm as a treasure hunt.

One chilly Saturday afternoon, Sam and I grabbed our woven baskets from the hall closet and raced outside, laughter trailing behind us. The wind had already scattered countless leaves across the lawn, creating a patchwork of color that crunched satisfyingly beneath our shoes.

"Bet I'll find the brightest red leaf," Sam shouted confidently, darting toward the maple tree that stood grandly at the edge of our yard. I laughed, feeling equally determined as I headed toward the towering oak near the fence.

We searched meticulously, kneeling close to the earth, sorting through piles of fallen leaves, hunting for the most vibrant colors and perfectly shaped edges. Occasionally, I'd glance up to see Sam holding a leaf high above his head, waving triumphantly. "I found one!" he'd call out, proudly displaying a leaf so red it seemed painted by hand.

Yet, I never lost hope. My eyes scanned carefully, finally discovering a golden leaf so large it could nearly cover my entire hand. I held it up, sunlight filtering through its delicate veins, and shouted back, "I've found the biggest golden leaf ever!"

We laughed and teased each other, quickly filling our baskets to overflowing. Our fingers grew chilled, but we barely noticed. The thrill of the competition kept us warm. Neighbors walking past stopped briefly, chuckling at our enthusiasm. Mrs. Murphy paused to admire our finds, telling us stories about when she and her siblings collected leaves long ago.

When our baskets were finally brimming with leaves, we hurried back home, racing toward the porch steps, each of us certain we'd won. Our parents would be the judges, carefully considering each leaf as though it were a priceless jewel, complimenting every color and shape. Mom pretended to deliberate seriously before declaring both baskets equally wonderful, prompting exaggerated groans and laughter from Sam and me.

After the judging, we'd dump all our collected leaves into one enormous pile in the backyard. Then, without hesitation, we'd leap into the leaves together, shrieking joyfully as bright colors exploded around us, floating gently back to earth. Our competition always ended the same way: tangled in laughter and covered in autumn's finest treasures.

Looking back, I realize those afternoons weren't really about winning or losing at all. They were about being together, sharing the simple joys of crisp air, colorful leaves, and playful adventures. To this day, whenever autumn arrives, I feel the familiar urge to gather leaves, remembering with warmth those playful contests and carefree days spent alongside my brother.

Memory Prompts:

- Did you ever collect leaves or pinecones in fall?
- Do you remember raking piles of leaves as a child?
- What autumn colors did you love most?

Conversation Starters:

- Do you enjoy autumn walks or spring strolls more?
- What's your favorite autumn activity?
- Would you rather keep a leaf as a souvenir or press flowers?

Thanksgiving Seat Swap

Thanksgiving dinners at our house were always lively and unpredictable affairs. The dining room, which rarely saw much action throughout the year, suddenly became the busiest place in the house. Mom laid out the best china, and Dad carefully carved the golden-brown turkey while family and friends gathered closely around the table, eagerly waiting for the meal to begin.

This particular Thanksgiving remains vivid in my memory because of what we later called "The Great Seat Swap." My mother had spent the entire morning arranging tiny name cards next to each plate, ensuring that everyone had the perfect seat. She believed seating arrangements were crucial to keeping peace during the family meal, especially between Uncle Joe, who talked nonstop, and Aunt Mildred, who preferred absolute quiet.

As guests arrived, bringing dishes of steaming vegetables, fresh bread rolls, and homemade pies, the house buzzed with cheerful greetings. But just as we prepared to sit, my young cousin Tommy decided to collect the pretty cards, reshuffling them gleefully in his hands like a deck of playing cards.

“Look! I’m helping!” Tommy declared proudly, scattering the name cards randomly back onto the table. Laughter erupted immediately, mixed with mild panic, as family members scrambled to find their new spots. Aunt Mildred suddenly found herself between my teenage cousins, who chattered endlessly about music she had never heard of. Uncle Joe somehow landed right next to my shy sister Laura, who usually hid quietly in a corner.

Initially, everyone looked uncertain, glancing around and chuckling nervously. But soon, the unexpected seating arrangement began to create unexpected connections. I watched in amusement as Uncle Joe managed to coax laughter from Laura with his funny childhood stories. Aunt Mildred, after initial bewilderment, found herself intrigued by the enthusiastic explanations of bands and singers she'd never encountered before. Even my grandmother, who preferred tradition above all else, began chatting animatedly with our neighbor Mr. Ellis, someone she'd never really spoken to at length before. The mix-up became a source of endless amusement, and as dishes passed from hand to hand, conversations bubbled up everywhere, filling the room with joyful chatter.

When Dad finally stood to make the toast, he raised his glass with a smile, eyes twinkling warmly. "To unexpected changes," he announced cheerfully. "May they always lead to moments like this—laughter, friendship, and love."

After dinner, as we sat together over slices of pumpkin and pecan pie, everyone agreed that Tommy's accidental reshuffle had made this Thanksgiving special. The laughter was louder, the smiles brighter, and friendships felt somehow deeper. Even Aunt Mildred, usually so particular about tradition, admitted she'd enjoyed herself immensely.

Every Thanksgiving afterward, my family jokingly debated whether to let Tommy rearrange the seats again. But beyond the laughter, we all secretly hoped he would, recognizing how even the smallest unexpected moments could create lasting joy. Now, years later, whenever I set the Thanksgiving table, I find myself smiling and thinking of Tommy's mischievous grin, reminding me that sometimes the best memories begin with an accidental swap.

Memory Prompts:

- Did your family have assigned seats at the table?
- Do you remember a holiday when someone unexpected showed up?
- What's the most memorable dish you enjoyed at Thanksgiving or another holiday?

Conversation Starters:

- Do you like big gatherings or smaller meals?
- What's your favorite part of a holiday meal?
- Do you enjoy cooking or simply tasting?

The New Year's Clock

In our family, New Year's Eve was always celebrated quietly, gathered around the old grandfather clock in the living room. That tall, sturdy clock had stood proudly in the corner for as long as I could remember, ticking steadily throughout each day, becoming part of our daily rhythm. Yet, on New Year's Eve, its role transformed into something special—something magical.

On that particular evening, my parents, grandparents, siblings, and I would settle comfortably in chairs pulled close together, wrapped in warm blankets, enjoying hot chocolate or tea. As midnight approached, excitement and anticipation filled the air. The television was off, replaced instead by soft conversation, stories, and laughter, all mingling gently with the steady, comforting tick-tock of our beloved clock.

One memorable New Year's Eve stands out clearly in my memory. It was nearing midnight, and we were all listening carefully, counting down the final moments. Grandpa, always precise about timing, had synchronized his wristwatch carefully, smiling in anticipation of the clock's resonant chime. My younger brother, Jimmy, sat eagerly at Grandpa's feet, eyes wide and bright, waiting for the first ring to mark the arrival of a fresh year.

As the minute hand finally reached twelve, we all leaned forward expectantly, breaths held. But instead of striking immediately, the old clock hesitated. Its familiar tick paused, as if the clock itself were caught up in the suspense. Then, almost comically late, the first chime finally rang out—strong, proud, and thoroughly off-time.

Laughter erupted spontaneously throughout the room. Even Grandma, who was typically reserved, began chuckling warmly. "Well," Grandpa said, smiling widely and glancing affectionately at the clock, "it looks like even the clock was unsure about leaving this year behind!"

We continued laughing through the remaining eleven chimes, now hopelessly out of rhythm but somehow even more endearing. The unexpected delay sparked playful teasing and good-natured jokes, making that year's countdown unforgettable. My mother gently hugged Jimmy, whispering softly in his ear, "See, sometimes life doesn't need to be perfect to be wonderful."

Once the final chime faded into silence, we raised our cups together, exchanging heartfelt wishes and resolutions. Grandpa's voice resonated softly through the quiet room as he raised his mug of tea and declared, "May the new year be as joyful, warm, and surprising as this evening has been!"

We nodded in agreement, savoring the simple joy of being together, embraced by warmth and laughter. That quirky grandfather clock, whose timing was far from perfect, had somehow captured exactly what our family loved most about celebrating a new year—embracing the unexpected and cherishing the imperfections.

Now, each year as midnight approaches, no matter where I am, my thoughts drift back to that cozy room filled with family, laughter, and our beloved, slightly off-time clock. It taught me something precious: that the sweetest moments often arrive in their own unexpected ways, perfectly imperfect, and warmly remembered forever.

Memory Prompts:

- Did your family stay up late on New Year's Eve?
- Do you remember a favorite New Year's tradition?
- Was there a year that felt extra special to welcome?

Conversation Starters:

- Do you prefer quiet New Year's evenings or lively parties?
- What's one tradition you'd bring back today?
- Do you enjoy fireworks, music, or countdowns more?

Summer Lemonade Stand

When summer arrived in our neighborhood, it meant long, sunlit days filled with bike rides, games in the yard, and, best of all, running our very own lemonade stand. My sister Katie and I spent weeks planning it, dreaming about the small fortune we were certain we would earn. We'd carefully craft signs with brightly colored letters and set aside a small table in the garage just for the occasion.

On the day we finally opened our stand, excitement woke us up earlier than usual. After breakfast, Mom helped us mix pitchers of lemonade, fresh lemons squeezed until our fingers tingled, sugar carefully stirred until perfectly dissolved. Katie placed chocolate chip cookies neatly on a plate, secretly sneaking a few extra for herself.

We carried everything carefully outside, arranging it on our little table near the sidewalk. Then we taped our signs to nearby trees, smiling proudly as neighbors waved from their porches, already promising to stop by.

Our first customers were Mr. and Mrs. Patterson, who smiled warmly and asked for two cups. Nervously, Katie poured lemonade into paper cups, spilling just a little as she handed them across the table. They insisted on paying double what we asked, telling us cheerfully, "Keep the change, young entrepreneurs!"

Encouraged, we shouted louder, "Ice-cold lemonade, fresh cookies!" Soon, more neighbors stopped by, each purchase making us happier and slightly more confident. Before long, our stand was bustling. Friends from down the street lined up patiently, coins jingling in their pockets, chatting excitedly about their summer plans.

But Katie, never the best at math, sometimes struggled counting out change. After one sale, she accidentally gave away an extra dollar in quarters, realizing her mistake only after the neighbor had already walked away. Her eyes widened in panic, but Dad laughed softly and reassured her, "Think of it as a tip for excellent service."

Another time, Katie proudly offered free cookies to Mrs. Jenkins, forgetting entirely that cookies were supposed to cost extra. I glanced at her in disbelief, but her happy grin was contagious, and soon I was smiling too, shaking my head and handing over another free cookie to the next customer, just to be fair.

As the afternoon heat rose, neighbors lingered, chatting under the shade of nearby trees, sipping lemonade and complimenting us on our refreshing drinks. The stand quickly became less about making money and more about creating something wonderful together. Friends brought chairs, laughing and sharing stories, turning our simple lemonade stand into an impromptu neighborhood gathering.

At day's end, counting our modest profits, Katie and I discovered we'd barely made enough to buy more lemons. Yet neither of us felt disappointed. Instead, we happily recounted our small triumphs and funny mistakes, realizing that the day had brought something far more valuable than coins—a sense of pride, community, and plenty of joyful laughter.

Even today, every time I sip ice-cold lemonade on a hot afternoon, I remember those warm summer days with Katie, the generosity of our neighbors, and the simple delight of childhood dreams.

Memory Prompts:

- Did you ever sell something as a child?
- Do you remember earning your first coins?
- Was there a treat you loved buying on hot days?

Conversation Starters:

- Do you prefer lemonade or iced tea in summer?
- Would you enjoy running a small stand today?
- What's your favorite way to cool off on a hot day?

Winter Carolers at the Door

On frosty December evenings, our neighborhood often grew quiet early, streets blanketed softly in fresh snow. The houses were cozy, their windows glowing warmly in the twilight, a comforting sight amid the cold. Yet, there was one winter night when the stillness was joyfully interrupted by the cheerful voices of carolers.

I clearly recall that particular evening, just days before Christmas, when my family had gathered in our living room. The fireplace crackled gently, filling the room with warmth, while we wrapped ourselves in blankets and sipped mugs of steaming cocoa. My sister, Emily, had just finished decorating the Christmas tree, proudly stepping back to admire her work. The house felt full of quiet anticipation for the holiday.

Then, suddenly, soft singing drifted faintly from outside. Curious, we hurried to the front window, pressing our faces close to the cold glass. There, beneath the glow of the streetlamp, stood a small group of neighbors bundled in scarves and coats, singing cheerfully. Their breath formed little clouds in the chilly air as they harmonized perfectly, voices blending beautifully in a classic carol.

Excitement filled the room. Emily pulled the front door open wide, letting in a rush of crisp winter air and joyful music. Standing in the doorway, we watched and listened, enchanted, clapping softly between songs. The carolers smiled warmly, their eyes sparkling with happiness as they launched into another familiar melody.

Soon, neighbors from nearby houses joined us, gathering around the carolers in a small crowd. Children giggled, parents exchanged smiles, and older neighbors quietly sang along, reminiscing fondly about winter evenings from their youth. Encouraged by the growing audience, the singers chose even livelier tunes, inviting us to join in. Before long, everyone—adults and children alike—was singing together, our voices rising joyfully into the snowy night.

I remember Mr. Harris, who rarely left his house due to the cold, stepping onto his porch wrapped in a thick blanket, smiling and humming along softly. Mrs. Campbell, from next door, clapped her mittened hands cheerfully, calling out requests for her favorite songs. The entire neighborhood felt alive, the cold forgotten as warmth and community filled the evening.

After a final, heartfelt chorus of "Silent Night," the carolers waved goodbye, their footsteps crunching softly in the snow as they moved toward the next house. We lingered in the doorway, calling out thanks and wishing them warm holidays. Returning indoors, we felt lighter, happier, and deeply connected to those around us.

In the quiet afterward, my family gathered again by the fireplace, smiling at each other with contentment. It wasn't just the songs that had lifted our spirits, but the feeling of togetherness they created, reminding us that even the coldest winter evenings could become special memories, filled with warmth, kindness, and simple joy.

Now, every December, when the first snow falls quietly outside my window, I pause, listening carefully, half expecting to hear the joyful sounds of carolers returning once more to our door.

Memory Prompts:

- Did you ever go caroling or hear singers at your door?
- Do you remember singing winter songs as a child?
- Was there a favorite holiday tune you loved?

Conversation Starters:

- Do you enjoy listening to choirs or solo voices more?
- What's your favorite holiday song?
- Would you rather sing or just listen?

The Family Reunion Quilt Signing

Family reunions in our household were always lively affairs, filled with hugs, laughter, delicious food, and endless storytelling. Yet one reunion stands out clearly in my memory, all because of a simple quilt—a quilt that became a cherished family treasure.

That particular summer, relatives traveled from near and far to gather at Aunt Clara's home, a spacious old farmhouse surrounded by green fields and gentle hills. On the day of the reunion, Aunt Clara surprised us by spreading a large quilt across the picnic table in the backyard. It was handmade, pieced carefully from colorful squares of fabric, each one unique and vibrant.

"Here's the idea," she announced brightly, handing out fabric markers. "Everyone signs their name on a square, and you can add a small message or memory. Next year, when we gather again, we'll read these notes and remember today."

Excitement filled the air as family members eagerly gathered around the table, markers in hand. At first, everyone hesitated, unsure of what to write, but soon laughter and cheerful conversation filled the backyard as creativity took hold.

My cousin Danny, always mischievous, drew a cartoon face beside his signature, prompting giggles from the younger children. Grandma Betty wrote carefully, adding a small heart and a simple message: "Family is forever." My father scribbled a funny joke he had told countless times, prompting playful groans from relatives who knew it by heart. Even shy Uncle Bill, usually quiet in large gatherings, smiled gently as he wrote his initials next to a small drawing of his favorite fishing rod.

As the afternoon continued, the quilt gradually filled with vibrant ink—each square capturing small glimpses of personality, stories, and memories. Aunt Clara walked among us, smiling warmly, pleased that her quilt had sparked such joy. Neighbors passing by stopped to admire our creation, some even signing their names on the corners, joining our family for just that day.

After a hearty meal and playful games, we gathered again to admire the quilt, now covered with colorful signatures, jokes, heartfelt messages, and small drawings. Aunt Clara carefully folded the quilt, promising to display it at every future reunion.

The following summer, true to her word, Aunt Clara again unfolded the quilt across the picnic table. Everyone crowded close, eager to find their squares. We laughed warmly, recalling jokes and stories from the previous year, amazed at how quickly the memories returned. New family members added their own messages, their squares joining seamlessly with ours.

That quilt soon became more than a piece of fabric—it was a living story of our family. Each reunion brought new signatures, memories, laughter, and sometimes gentle tears. Even as years passed and faces changed, the quilt connected us, reminding us that our family bond was woven tightly, stitched by moments of love and shared joy.

Today, when I picture that quilt, I see more than colorful squares and scribbled names. I see Aunt Clara's gentle smile, hear Grandma Betty's laughter, feel the warmth of endless summer days, and remember clearly that family, above all else, is the greatest treasure we carry in our hearts.

Memory Prompts:

- Did your family hold reunions or large get-togethers?
- Do you remember signing or creating something together?
- Was there a keepsake from your family gatherings?

Conversation Starters:

- Would you rather attend a picnic reunion or a banquet?
- What family tradition do you cherish most?
- Do you enjoy looking at old family keepsakes?

Chapter 8: Life Lessons

Life often teaches its most valuable lessons through quiet, unexpected moments. This chapter shares gentle stories about experiences we can all relate to, like forgetting homework and discovering kindness in a teacher's encouragement, or misplacing something important and learning gratitude when a stranger returns it. Perhaps you recall breaking a precious family item as a child, only to be met with forgiveness instead of anger, or accidentally taking the wrong train ticket and ending up somewhere new and wonderful. These small yet powerful experiences remind us how mistakes and misunderstandings often lead to growth and understanding. As you read, think about times when someone's patience or compassion changed your perspective, maybe through a heartfelt apology, a helpful neighbor, or a humorous misunderstanding. Life's most meaningful lessons are often hidden within everyday moments, teaching us compassion, honesty, and humility when we least expect it. Allow yourself to recall your own simple yet memorable encounters, those experiences that taught you something valuable or left you feeling wiser. These stories will gently guide you through memories that shaped you, comforted you, or simply reminded you how kindness, humor, and forgiveness make life truly rewarding.

The Forgotten Homework

Emily's heart dropped as she stared into her backpack. It was like her math homework had simply vanished. She had spent all evening carefully working through the problems, double-checking her answers, and placing it neatly into her folder. But now, the folder was empty, and a panic settled in her chest.

Glancing around, she saw her classmates pulling out their completed assignments, ready to hand them to Mrs. Thompson, their teacher. Emily's cheeks burned hot as she desperately shuffled through her bag again, hoping the homework had simply hidden itself between textbooks or loose pages. But each search turned up empty.

Emily was rarely forgetful, and schoolwork was important to her. She wanted her teachers to think highly of her, and she hated disappointing anyone. As Mrs. Thompson walked from desk to desk collecting the assignments, Emily's anxiety rose.

Soon enough, Mrs. Thompson reached Emily's desk, looking down expectantly. "Emily?"

Emily took a shaky breath and confessed quietly, "I—I can't find my homework. I swear I did it, Mrs. Thompson, but it's not here."

She braced herself for the teacher's reaction, anticipating a look of disappointment, maybe even frustration. But instead, Mrs. Thompson gently placed her hand on Emily's desk and smiled softly.

"I understand, Emily," she said calmly. "Sometimes things just slip our minds or get misplaced. Why don't you look for it again tonight and bring it tomorrow? I trust you."

Emily felt tears prick the corners of her eyes, not from embarrassment, but from relief and gratitude. She hadn't expected kindness. Mrs. Thompson's gentle reaction made Emily feel lighter, almost as if a weight had lifted from her shoulders.

The rest of the day passed smoothly, but Emily couldn't stop reflecting on Mrs. Thompson's kindness. She had shown Emily compassion when she had expected criticism, and that felt incredibly special. That moment stayed with her far longer than any math assignment would have.

From that day forward, Emily carried Mrs. Thompson's lesson in patience and understanding with her, long after she moved on to other grades and schools. Eventually, Emily grew up and found herself in Mrs. Thompson's shoes, teaching her own classroom of young students.

One crisp autumn morning, a quiet boy named Jacob sat at his desk, anxiously digging through his backpack. Emily recognized his panicked expression immediately. She knew exactly what had happened even before Jacob raised his hand.

"I can't find my homework," Jacob admitted quietly, his voice barely audible.

Emily knelt beside his desk and smiled warmly. "That's okay, Jacob. I believe you did it. Just bring it in tomorrow."

Jacob's eyes brightened with relief, and Emily remembered exactly how good it felt to receive kindness instead of criticism. As Jacob relaxed, Emily thought again of Mrs. Thompson and silently thanked her for teaching a lesson that was about much more than math. It was about compassion, patience, and the lifelong impact a simple, kind gesture could make.

Memory Prompts:

- Did you ever forget to bring something important to school?
- Do you remember a teacher who showed you patience?
- Was there a time someone surprised you with understanding?

Conversation Starters:

- Do you think mistakes help us learn more than success?
- What advice would you give a student today?
- Did you prefer strict or gentle teachers?

The Lost Wallet

Benjamin had just stepped off the city bus when he felt a sinking feeling. His hand automatically reached for his back pocket, but the comforting shape of his wallet wasn't there. His stomach tightened with worry as he quickly checked every other pocket. Nothing. A wave of frustration and anxiety washed over him as he retraced his steps mentally, picturing exactly where it might have fallen.

He paced back and forth along the sidewalk, scanning the ground and hoping to spot the familiar brown leather. But with each passing minute, the chances of finding it grew slimmer. He sighed deeply, realizing the wallet was probably already in someone else's hands. His hard-earned money, identification, and family photos—all gone in an instant.

Feeling defeated, Benjamin headed home, his shoulders heavy with disappointment. As he walked, he thought of all the times his parents had warned him to be careful. Their voices echoed in his head, causing him to blame himself even more.

At dinner, Benjamin was quiet. His family asked if something was wrong, but he hesitated to tell them about the wallet. Eventually, he explained everything, embarrassed about the mistake he'd made. His father reassured him gently, telling him it could happen to anyone. Still, Benjamin could hardly sleep that night, thinking about the consequences of losing something so important.

The following morning, Benjamin was surprised by a knock at the door. Opening it, he saw an elderly man with a kind face standing on the porch, holding something familiar. Benjamin's heart leaped.

"I think this might belong to you," the man said with a gentle smile, extending the wallet toward Benjamin.

Benjamin was speechless. "You—you found it?" he stammered.

The man nodded warmly. "I spotted it near the bus stop yesterday afternoon. It had your address inside, and I figured you'd be worried."

Benjamin took the wallet with trembling hands. Everything was still inside, exactly as he'd left it. His voice filled with gratitude, he tried to thank the man, offering to give him something in return. But the elderly stranger simply shook his head, smiling.

"No need, young man. Just promise me you'll pass along the kindness someday."

As the man walked away down the sidewalk, Benjamin stood in the doorway, amazed by the stranger's honesty and generosity. His lost wallet was back, but what touched him even more deeply was the kindness he'd just experienced.

In the days and weeks that followed, Benjamin found himself thinking often about that elderly man. He became more aware of those around him who needed help, offering small gestures of kindness whenever he could. He returned dropped items, helped neighbors carry groceries, and held doors open for strangers. Each simple action reminded him of the gentle promise he'd made.

Years later, Benjamin still told the story of the lost wallet—not because he remembered the panic, but because he'd never forgotten the kindness. The stranger's generosity had taught him something valuable: small gestures, even those as simple as returning a lost wallet, have the power to restore our faith in others and inspire us to pass kindness forward.

Memory Prompts:

- Have you ever lost something valuable and gotten it back?
- Do you remember a stranger showing you kindness?
- Did you ever return something that wasn't yours?

Conversation Starters:

- Do you believe most people are honest?
- What would you do if you found a wallet today?
- Do you think small good deeds make a big difference?

The Wrong Train Ticket

Julia clutched her train ticket tightly, her eyes darting anxiously between the departure board and the crowded station platform. She was taking a weekend trip to visit her sister and had double-checked the timetable carefully—at least, she thought she had. As passengers hurried around her, a sudden sense of unease crept in. Something felt off.

When the train pulled into the station, she climbed aboard and found a seat by the window. The scenery outside blurred into fields and farms, eventually shifting into unfamiliar countryside. After an hour passed, Julia's worry deepened. Nothing looked familiar.

"Excuse me," she asked a woman seated nearby, "is this the train to Brooksville?"

The woman raised her eyebrows in gentle surprise. "Brooksville? No, dear, we're headed to Redfield."

Julia’s stomach twisted into a knot. She'd bought the wrong ticket, boarded the wrong train, and was now traveling in the opposite direction from her intended destination. Embarrassment flushed her cheeks as she fumbled for her phone, realizing she'd soon have to explain this silly mistake to her sister.

But as she glanced around nervously, trying to hide her embarrassment, the woman next to her gently placed a reassuring hand on her arm. "Don't worry," she said kindly. "We've all been there. Maybe there's a reason you're here instead."

The woman introduced herself as Anne, and as they began to chat, Julia felt her anxiety fading. Anne spoke warmly about Redfield, describing its charming shops, peaceful parks, and friendly people. She even recommended a café known for delicious pastries and strong coffee.

When the train finally stopped at Redfield station, Anne invited Julia to join her for coffee, offering her company and comfort in this unexpected detour. Julia, feeling grateful for the warmth of this new friendship, happily accepted.

They spent the afternoon strolling through Redfield’s picturesque streets, chatting about their lives, sharing laughter and discovering how much they had in common. What had started as an embarrassing mistake turned into one of Julia’s most enjoyable afternoons in recent memory.

As the daylight faded, Anne walked Julia back to the station, helping her buy the correct ticket to Brooksville. As Julia stepped onto the evening train, she hugged Anne warmly, feeling as though she'd known her much longer than a few hours.

When Julia finally arrived at her sister's home late that evening, she wasn't focused on the inconvenience of the delay or the stress of getting lost. Instead, she excitedly shared her unexpected adventure and the friendship that had blossomed out of her mistake.

From that day forward, Julia often reflected on her wrong train ticket—not as an error, but as proof of life's unexpected kindness. She’d learned that a journey isn’t always about getting exactly where you're supposed to be, but sometimes about ending up exactly where you need to be.

Memory Prompts:

- Did you ever take a train trip to a new place?
- Do you recall a time when a mistake turned into something good?
- Was there a stranger you met who left a lasting impression?

Conversation Starters:

- Do you prefer planned trips or spontaneous ones?
- What’s a journey you’d like to take again?
- Do you enjoy traveling by train, bus, or car the most?

The Broken Vase

Lucas stood frozen in the middle of the living room, staring down at the shattered pieces of his mother's favorite porcelain vase scattered across the wooden floor. His heartbeat quickened, and a cold wave of dread washed over him. He'd been warned countless times to be careful when playing indoors, and now he'd made a mistake he couldn't hide.

With shaky hands, Lucas began picking up the broken fragments. He imagined the disappointment on his mother's face when she discovered what he'd done. The vase had been passed down from his grandmother, a precious family heirloom. Lucas felt tears filling his eyes as he tried, unsuccessfully, to put the pieces back together.

Just as he was about to give up, he heard the familiar sound of the front door opening and closing. His stomach knotted as his mother walked into the room, stopping immediately when she saw Lucas kneeling on the floor, tears rolling down his cheeks.

"I'm sorry, Mom," Lucas stammered, barely able to look up. "I didn't mean to break it—I just wasn't careful enough."

His mother stood quietly for a moment, taking in the scene. Lucas braced himself for anger, a harsh scolding, or at least disappointment. But instead, his mother slowly knelt beside him and softly placed her hand on his shoulder.

"Are you hurt?" she asked gently.

Surprised by her calmness, Lucas shook his head. "No, I'm fine. But your vase..."

His mother smiled softly and squeezed his shoulder. "It's just an object, Lucas. It meant a lot to me because of the memories attached to it—not because it was perfect or unbroken."

Lucas stared at her in disbelief, relief washing over him. His mother's kindness was unexpected and comforting, and he suddenly felt even worse for causing her pain.

Noticing his continued distress, his mother continued, "Accidents happen, Lucas. Objects break, but our family bond doesn't. I'm just glad you're not hurt."

Together, they gathered the fragments carefully, deciding to keep them in a special box as a reminder that things could break but love and understanding could remain intact. Lucas learned something important that day—not about porcelain or vases, but about compassion and forgiveness. He saw clearly how choosing kindness over anger could mend even the sharpest hurts.

Years later, Lucas still remembered that moment vividly. As he grew older, he carried that lesson with him, guiding him in moments when frustration and anger might have been easier responses. And when, many years later, his own daughter accidentally broke his favorite coffee mug, he smiled warmly, knelt beside her, and gently reassured her in the very same way his mother had once comforted him.

That broken vase had taught Lucas that mistakes didn't have to separate families; sometimes, they could bring people closer together, connected by compassion, understanding, and a lasting bond of forgiveness.

Memory Prompts:

- Did you ever break something important at home?
- Do you remember a time you were forgiven for a mistake?
- Was there an object in your home that felt precious?

Conversation Starters:

- Do you think mistakes can bring families closer?
- What would you say to comfort someone who made a mistake?
- Do you prefer keeping fragile things on display or stored safely?

The Apology Note

Daniel sat at his small desk, staring at the blank piece of paper in front of him. His hand hovered uncertainly above it, gripping a blue pen that felt suddenly heavy. He knew what he wanted to say, but every time he tried to start writing, embarrassment and doubt crept in, stopping him cold.

Earlier that day, Daniel had argued with his best friend, Robbie, over something trivial—a misunderstanding about whose turn it was in a neighborhood baseball game. The disagreement quickly turned sour, ending with harsh words neither truly meant. Daniel regretted it almost immediately, and his stomach twisted whenever he remembered the hurt expression on Robbie's face.

Realizing he couldn't leave things unresolved, Daniel finally pressed the pen to paper, carefully forming each letter:

"Robbie, I'm really sorry about today. I shouldn't have gotten so angry. I didn't mean what I said. You're my best friend, and our friendship matters more than any game. Please forgive me."

After finishing, Daniel read the note several times, feeling nervous but relieved. He carefully folded it, placing it into a small envelope with Robbie's name neatly printed on the front. Slipping out quietly, Daniel walked two houses down the street, his heart pounding with uncertainty as he gently dropped the envelope through Robbie's mailbox slot.

The next morning, Daniel woke early, anxious about Robbie's reaction. Would he accept the apology, or would their friendship remain broken? His worries intensified during breakfast, each minute dragging slowly.

Then the doorbell rang. Daniel hurried to answer, his pulse quickening as he opened the door. Robbie stood there, smiling sheepishly, holding the note in one hand.

"I got your letter," Robbie said softly. "Thanks for saying sorry. I'm sorry too."

Instantly, Daniel felt the weight lift from his shoulders. Robbie had forgiven him, just as he'd hoped. Without another word, they exchanged smiles that said everything important, mending their friendship in a quiet moment of understanding.

That simple apology taught Daniel something powerful about forgiveness. From then on, whenever misunderstandings or conflicts arose, Daniel remembered the quiet courage it took to write those simple words, "I'm sorry," and how much healing power they carried. Over the years, he kept the memory close, allowing it to guide him through countless disagreements and misunderstandings, reminding him how a sincere apology could heal even the deepest wounds.

Decades later, Daniel still cherished that early lesson. When his granddaughter came home upset after a disagreement with her friend, he gently encouraged her to write a short note. "Words from the heart can mend anything," he explained kindly, watching her carefully write out an apology, just as he once had. He smiled softly, remembering that long-ago moment when simple, humble words had shown him exactly how much power and warmth could live inside a handwritten apology.

Memory Prompts:

- Did you ever write or receive an apology?
- Do you remember a time a letter solved a problem?
- Who taught you the importance of saying “sorry”?

Conversation Starters:

- Do you think apologies should be spoken or written?
- What makes an apology feel sincere to you?
- Have you ever received a meaningful note?

The Forgotten Name

Olivia stood awkwardly near the snack table at her niece's wedding, sipping lemonade and hoping no one would notice how out-of-place she felt. She smiled politely as a cheerful woman approached, waving excitedly.

"Olivia! It's so wonderful to see you again," the woman said warmly, her eyes sparkling with recognition.

Olivia's heart jumped. She knew the woman's face instantly, but her name was completely lost. She scrambled through her memory, trying desperately to find it. "Oh! Hello there," she managed to reply, smiling a bit too widely.

The woman continued to chat comfortably, mentioning shared memories from past family gatherings. Olivia nodded, laughed, and responded vaguely, feeling increasingly uneasy. The woman's name still wouldn't come. She felt a blush rising, embarrassment washing over her as she silently urged her brain to cooperate.

Finally, seeing Olivia's discomfort, the woman gently touched her arm and laughed softly. "Olivia, you've completely forgotten my name, haven't you?"

Olivia hesitated, then sighed deeply and nodded, blushing even brighter. "I'm so sorry. I know I should know it."

Instead of taking offense, the woman laughed warmly. "Please don't worry," she said reassuringly. "It's Claire. Honestly, I've done the same thing myself many times. Names just escape us sometimes, don't they?"

Olivia let out a relieved breath and smiled gratefully. Claire's understanding dissolved the embarrassment immediately, and soon both women were laughing freely about their shared forgetfulness.

Throughout the wedding reception, Olivia and Claire stayed close, joking and swapping stories about other humorous memory lapses they'd experienced over the years. They discovered they had plenty in common besides just forgetting names. By the end of the evening, Olivia felt she'd made a true friend.

On the way home, Olivia reflected on what had started as an embarrassing mistake but ended as a joyful encounter. She realized that admitting a simple lapse of memory had allowed both women to relax and enjoy themselves, forging an unexpected bond through honesty and humor.

Years passed, but Olivia never forgot Claire again, and their friendship blossomed from that funny, honest moment at the wedding. They often joked about how their friendship had begun with Olivia's forgotten name, recognizing how honesty had set them free from embarrassment.

Eventually, Olivia learned to handle forgetfulness with ease, laughing gently at herself instead of worrying. She understood now that small mistakes like forgetting someone's name could actually open doors to friendship and connection if met with openness rather than embarrassment.

One afternoon, as Olivia met her granddaughter's new friend, she sensed the young girl struggling to remember her name. She quickly stepped in, smiling warmly. "Don't worry, dear," she said kindly. "I'm Olivia. And believe me, forgetting a name just means you're human."

The young girl relaxed, smiling gratefully. Olivia glanced across the room, catching Claire's eyes and sharing a quiet laugh, reminded once again how the smallest moments of kindness and humor could grow into lifelong friendships.

Memory Prompts:

- Did you ever forget a name at the wrong time?
- Do you remember meeting someone important unexpectedly?
- Was there a funny mix-up you experienced with names?

Conversation Starters:

- Do you prefer remembering names or faces more easily?
- What helps you recall people you meet?
- Would you enjoy being called by a nickname?

The Shared Umbrella of Friendship

Maggie and Katie walked to school together every morning, laughing, chatting, and enjoying the simple routines of their friendship. Usually, their conversations flowed smoothly, punctuated by giggles and whispers. But today was different. Today, they were silent, their steps stiff and deliberate, each avoiding the other's eyes.

Earlier that morning, the two friends had gotten into an argument over a small misunderstanding—nothing terribly serious, but enough to leave hurt feelings on both sides. Now, walking separately along the same sidewalk felt strange and uncomfortable.

Suddenly, Maggie felt a raindrop splash onto her forehead, followed by another, and soon a steady drizzle soaked the sidewalk ahead. Maggie sighed, remembering that her umbrella was sitting on the kitchen table at home.

She quickened her pace, trying to avoid the rain, but soon felt the drops soaking through her jacket. Just then, she heard hurried footsteps approaching from behind, and Katie appeared beside her, holding out a large yellow umbrella.

"Here," Katie said softly, almost shyly, "I have room under my umbrella if you want."

Maggie hesitated for a brief moment, then quickly nodded. The two girls moved closer together beneath the bright canopy, shoulders nearly touching. At first, neither said anything, listening to the gentle tapping of rain above them. The silence stretched awkwardly until Maggie finally spoke.

"I'm sorry, Katie," she whispered. "I didn't mean to upset you earlier."

Katie immediately shook her head, looking relieved. "I'm sorry too. I shouldn't have gotten so angry about something small."

Under the shared umbrella, with the rain gently falling around them, the tension faded. Soon their conversation was easy again, the earlier disagreement melting away. They laughed softly, joking about the sudden rain, feeling closer because they'd both made an effort to forgive.

By the time they reached the school gates, the rain had slowed, leaving puddles shimmering on the pavement. Maggie smiled gratefully at her friend as Katie shook off the umbrella. The simple gesture had changed their entire morning, mending their friendship and teaching them something important about kindness and forgiveness.

Years later, Maggie often thought about that rainy morning—the cold drops of rain, the warm yellow umbrella, and the comfort of being forgiven. She understood now that arguments between friends didn't matter nearly as much as the willingness to reach out and forgive each other.

One afternoon, when her granddaughter returned home from school upset over a disagreement with her best friend, Maggie smiled gently and shared her story. "Sometimes friendship just needs a little shelter from the rain," she said softly. "And kindness is like sharing an umbrella. It doesn't just keep you dry; it brings you closer."

Her granddaughter listened carefully, her expression thoughtful. The next morning, Maggie watched proudly from the porch as her granddaughter offered a bright red umbrella to her waiting friend. She smiled to herself, remembering the yellow umbrella and how one small gesture of kindness could heal friendships, one raindrop at a time.

Memory Prompts:

- Did you ever make up with a friend after an argument?
- Do you remember walking with a friend in the rain?
- Was there a time kindness changed a friendship?

Conversation Starters:

- Do you prefer rainy walks or sunny strolls?
- How do you show kindness to a friend today?
- What's the best thing a friend has done for you?

The Misdelivered Letter

Laura had just finished watering her garden when she noticed the mail carrier slipping letters into her mailbox. Wiping her hands dry, she walked over, smiling warmly as she waved hello. Gathering the stack of mail, she flipped through envelopes and magazines until one particular letter caught her eye. The name on the envelope wasn't hers—it belonged to someone named Dorothy Simmons.

Laura glanced again at the address. Dorothy's house was just three doors down, and although they'd often waved politely, they'd never really spoken beyond occasional greetings. Laura hesitated only a moment, deciding it was best to deliver the letter personally. She walked along the sidewalk toward Dorothy's porch, feeling slightly shy about approaching her neighbor's home for the first time.

As she reached the house, Laura knocked softly on the door. A moment later, Dorothy appeared, her eyes brightening when she recognized Laura.

"Hello, Laura! What a nice surprise," Dorothy said, her smile warm and welcoming.

Laura held out the envelope apologetically. "Hi, Dorothy. The mail carrier accidentally gave me your letter."

Dorothy chuckled softly as she took the envelope. "Thank you so much for bringing it over. Would you like to come in for some tea? I've just put the kettle on."

Laura hesitated briefly, then nodded, smiling at Dorothy's gentle invitation. Inside, the house was cozy, filled with books, potted plants, and the inviting aroma of freshly brewed tea. Sitting at Dorothy's small kitchen table, the two women began to talk, quickly discovering they shared many interests and similar life experiences.

The letter, which had seemed merely a misdelivered piece of mail, had sparked an unexpected friendship. They talked effortlessly for hours, trading stories and laughter over cups of steaming tea. Laura felt entirely at ease in Dorothy's company, wondering why it had taken a simple mix-up for them to finally connect.

From that day on, Laura and Dorothy met regularly. They shared recipes, swapped gardening tips, and often enjoyed quiet afternoons chatting comfortably over tea. Each conversation deepened their friendship, proving how even the smallest acts of neighborly kindness could grow into something lasting and meaningful.

Years later, Laura often smiled as she remembered the accidental letter delivery. She was grateful for that small postal mistake, because it had shown her the value hidden in everyday gestures, reminding her how friendship could blossom unexpectedly, starting with something as simple as returning misdelivered mail.

One afternoon, Laura's grandson picked up a letter mistakenly left in their mailbox. Looking up at her, he asked curiously, "Should we give it back?"

Laura smiled warmly, nodding. "Absolutely. You never know, it might be the beginning of a wonderful friendship."

Taking his hand, Laura walked with him down the street, remembering Dorothy's welcoming smile. She knew firsthand how much warmth and kindness could flow from a simple, thoughtful gesture.

Memory Prompts:

- Did you ever receive someone else's mail?
- Do you remember helping a neighbor in small ways?
- Did anyone ever do a kind favor for you without asking?

Conversation Starters:

- Do you prefer writing letters or making phone calls?
- What's a small favor you enjoy doing for others?
- Do you like sending postcards when traveling?

The Misread Recipe

Martha glanced confidently at the cookbook resting open on the kitchen counter. She and her neighbor, Helen, had decided to bake a special cake for their neighborhood holiday gathering, excited about surprising everyone with a homemade treat. They both prided themselves on being careful cooks, known among friends and family for their delicious meals.

As they began mixing ingredients, they chatted cheerfully, passing the flour, eggs, and butter back and forth. Helen read the ingredients aloud, while Martha measured carefully. Distracted by their laughter and comfortable conversation, Martha mistakenly reached for salt instead of sugar. Neither woman noticed the mistake, and they cheerfully mixed and poured the batter into the pan, placing it carefully in the oven.

Soon, the kitchen filled with a delightful aroma. Helen smiled happily. "It smells delicious, Martha. Everyone's going to love it."

But when Martha opened the oven to check the cake, she paused. "It doesn't look quite right," she said uncertainly. Helen leaned over her shoulder, eyebrows furrowing at the odd texture.

Removing the cake from the oven, Martha nervously tasted a tiny piece, her face immediately twisting into confusion. "Oh dear," she murmured, realizing instantly what had happened. "I think I mixed up the sugar and salt!"

Helen laughed gently, tasting a piece herself, quickly agreeing that the cake was more salty than sweet. Martha's cheeks flushed red, embarrassment creeping in. She had wanted everything to be perfect.

Just then, Helen took another small bite, thoughtful for a moment. "You know what, Martha? It's not exactly what we planned, but with a bit of cream cheese and herbs, this could actually make a delicious savory snack!"

Martha smiled, grateful for Helen's kindness and optimism. Together, they quickly prepared a savory spread, decorating the cake slices beautifully. When they brought the unexpected dish to the neighborhood gathering, their friends hesitated at first, curious and slightly amused. But after one bite, faces lit up in delighted surprise.

"Delicious!" one neighbor exclaimed, reaching eagerly for another piece. "This is so tasty. What a clever idea!"

Soon, everyone was praising their accidental creation. Martha and Helen exchanged smiles, relief washing over them as they joined the laughter. What had started as a mistake had become the star of the evening.

Afterward, the two women sat in Martha's cozy kitchen, reflecting happily over cups of tea. Helen smiled warmly, saying, "Sometimes the best recipes happen by mistake, don't they?"

Martha nodded, laughing softly. "Yes, and sometimes mistakes taste better than what we originally planned."

Over the years, Martha often told the story of their misread recipe, always remembering the laughter, friendship, and unexpected success that followed a simple mix-up in the kitchen. It taught her that not every mistake had to be disappointing—sometimes, mistakes could lead to something wonderful, bringing laughter, creativity, and unforgettable memories.

Memory Prompts:

- Did you ever cook with friends or neighbors?
- Do you remember a meal that didn't turn out as planned?
- Was there a time you laughed over a cooking mishap?

Conversation Starters:

- Do you prefer cooking with others or alone?
- What's a dish you'd love to try making together?
- Do you enjoy sweet recipes or savory ones more?

The Surprise Toast

Anna had always been quiet, someone who preferred to listen rather than speak. At family dinners, she usually sat quietly, smiling gently and letting others take the spotlight. But tonight was special: her granddaughter Caroline was celebrating her engagement, and Anna wanted to share something meaningful.

The dinner was lively, the table set beautifully with flowers and candles, dishes passed around amid cheerful chatter. Anna watched quietly, feeling the warmth and joy surrounding her family. Her hand trembled slightly as she reached for the small glass in front of her, taking a calming breath.

As conversation paused, she slowly stood, her heart beating faster as all eyes turned to her. The room became silent, and Anna felt a flutter of nerves—but seeing Caroline's curious, affectionate smile steadied her courage.

“I don’t usually speak up,” Anna began softly, smiling shyly. “But tonight, I have something I want to share.”

Her family looked at her with surprise and curiosity, leaning in to hear better.

Anna took a slow breath, steadying herself. “Caroline, when I was your age, your grandfather and I had very little. But we always had laughter, kindness, and love. Those were the greatest treasures of our lives.”

She paused, her voice gaining strength as her memories flooded warmly back. “The secret to a joyful life isn’t money or possessions—it’s choosing kindness every single day. Your grandfather taught me that.”

Anna’s eyes sparkled softly, thinking of him, and her voice became stronger, filled with gentle humor. “He also taught me never to take life too seriously. Once, he tried to cook dinner for our anniversary and nearly burned the kitchen down. But that dinner is still my favorite memory because we laughed so hard together.”

The family chuckled affectionately, smiles widening at the memory she shared. Caroline's eyes shone brightly, touched by her grandmother's words.

Anna raised her glass gently, smiling with quiet confidence. "Tonight, Caroline, as you and Daniel look toward your future, I hope you fill your life with kindness, laughter, and forgiveness, even in the moments that don't go perfectly. Because those are the moments that will truly define your love."

As Anna finished her toast, the room filled with warmth and applause. Caroline rose quickly, rushing over to hug her grandmother, tears of joy in her eyes.

Later, as guests began to leave, Caroline sat beside Anna, squeezing her hand gently. "Grandma, your toast meant everything to me. I didn't know you could speak so beautifully!"

Anna laughed softly, eyes twinkling. "Neither did I, dear. But love gives us courage."

Years later, family members often recalled Anna's surprise toast with affection, remembering how her heartfelt words brought everyone closer that night. Anna's quiet courage had taught them all a gentle lesson: even a shy voice could deliver powerful words, bringing warmth and wisdom to those they loved most.

Memory Prompts:

- Did you ever give a speech or toast?
- Do you remember someone surprising you with kind words?
- Was there a family dinner that felt unforgettable?

Conversation Starters:

- Do you enjoy listening to speeches or stories at events?
- If you gave a toast today, what would you say?
- Do you prefer serious words or funny ones in a toast?

Chapter 9: Adventures & Travel

Travel opens our eyes to new experiences and gently pushes us beyond our everyday routines. Often, the most memorable journeys aren't carefully planned but are instead full of spontaneous moments, friendly encounters, and unexpected detours that lead to laughter. Maybe you recall a scenic train ride through breathtaking mountain landscapes, sharing stories and snacks with fellow travelers, or perhaps a family road trip where a wrong turn led to discovering a charming little town. Sometimes, adventure found us closer to home, in seaside visits building sandcastles, in the playful chaos of packing suitcases, or following a map that amusingly led nowhere but still created lasting memories. As you read these stories, take a moment to think of your own travels, big or small. Reflect on moments spent chatting with friendly strangers, laughing over misplaced luggage, or savoring local dishes that later became personal favorites. Travel isn't just about reaching a destination but about enjoying the small moments along the way. Let these stories softly remind you that the greatest adventures often come from simple, everyday experiences that stay with us forever, gently reminding us of the places we've been and the friendships we've made.

The Train to the Mountains

Emma had dreamed of this train ride for years. Ever since she was a girl, she'd imagined looking out from the window of a train, watching as green fields turned into towering mountains. Now, finally, she was on board, ticket in hand, ready to make the journey she'd long anticipated.

Inside the train car, there was a pleasant hum of conversation. Emma found a window seat and settled in comfortably, pulling out her small bag filled with snacks for the journey. Across from her sat an older couple, smiling warmly and already chatting with the passengers nearby. She liked them immediately.

As the train pulled out of the station, the city began to shrink behind them. Soon, lush hills appeared, rolling softly, as if painted in shades of emerald. Emma watched in quiet amazement as sheep dotted the hillsides and small cottages appeared tucked away in valleys. The older couple across the aisle opened a box of homemade cookies and passed them around, offering Emma one with a gentle nod.

"I baked them myself," the woman said, her voice kind and inviting. Emma accepted gladly, savoring the buttery sweetness as she admired the scenery.

"Is this your first time heading to the mountains?" asked a young man sitting nearby. He had a friendly face, his eyes bright with curiosity.

"Yes," Emma replied, smiling. "I've always dreamed of seeing the peaks up close. Have you been before?"

He nodded eagerly. "Every year since I was a kid. My grandfather used to take me hiking. There's nothing quite like it. You'll love it."

The conversation flowed naturally, drawing in others who shared their own mountain stories—memories of camping trips, sunrise hikes, and evenings spent by warm fires. Emma felt a growing sense of camaraderie as the passengers shared snacks and laughter, the train gently rocking as it climbed higher.

Then, as if appearing by magic, the first snow-capped peaks came into view, majestic and glittering in the afternoon sun. Gasps of delight filled the car as passengers leaned toward the windows, taking in the breathtaking sight. The train wound through tunnels carved into rock, emerging each time to more astonishing vistas.

Emma pressed her face close to the cool glass, absorbing the beauty of towering pine trees and sheer cliffs dropping dramatically beside them. The older woman across the aisle caught her eye, smiling knowingly. "It's even better than I remember," she said, her voice tinged with wonder.

Soon, a conductor came through, announcing their arrival was near. Passengers slowly packed their belongings, exchanging friendly goodbyes and promises to meet again on return journeys. Emma felt a gentle tug of sadness at the thought of the trip ending but quickly reminded herself that the adventure had only begun.

Stepping off the train, she took a deep breath of crisp mountain air. Surrounded by fellow travelers, all smiling and chatting excitedly, Emma realized something important: the journey itself, filled with unexpected friendship and shared laughter, had been just as beautiful as the stunning mountain views.

Memory Prompts:

- Did you ever travel to the mountains?
- Do you remember your first long train ride?
- Was there a trip that felt full of adventure?

Conversation Starters:

- Do you prefer mountain trips or beach holidays?
- What’s the most beautiful view you’ve seen from a window?
- Would you rather travel by train or boat?

The Wrong Turn on the Road Trip

They had been driving for hours, and despite the careful planning and maps, they still managed to make a wrong turn somewhere outside a small town they'd never heard of before. Tom glanced over at his wife, Carol, who was squinting at the outdated map unfolded across her lap.

"I think we missed a turn about ten miles back," she said with a sigh, glancing around at the unfamiliar fields and farmhouses passing by the windows.

Their two grandkids, Sophie and Ben, who had been chattering and giggling in the backseat, now leaned forward curiously.

"Are we lost?" Ben asked eagerly, his voice brimming with excitement.

Carol smiled, shaking her head gently. "No, honey. We're just on a bit of an adventure."

Tom chuckled, sensing her quiet frustration beneath the cheerful tone. "Maybe we'll ask someone up ahead."

Soon, colorful banners and a lively crowd appeared up ahead, filling the usually quiet main street. Tom slowed down, rolling down the window to listen to the cheerful music drifting through the air. People milled around stalls selling popcorn, cotton candy, and handcrafted toys. A local band played spirited songs from a makeshift stage, the upbeat rhythm inviting everyone to join in the festivities.

"A fair!" Sophie exclaimed, pressing her nose against the glass. "Can we stop? Please, Grandpa?"

Tom glanced at Carol, whose frustration had melted away at the unexpected sight. She nodded, eyes sparkling. "Why not? We're already here."

They parked near the edge of the festivities and climbed out, the scent of fried dough and roasted corn filling the warm air. Tom and Carol watched as the grandkids dashed toward a colorful carousel, laughter bubbling from them like music.

As they walked through the fair, townspeople greeted them warmly, inviting them to taste homemade pies, admire intricate quilts, and join games like ring-toss and sack races. Tom found himself chatting comfortably with a vendor selling carved wooden toys, while Carol admired a table filled with hand-sewn aprons.

"See, Grandma?" Sophie said, skipping up with a cotton candy cone nearly as big as she was. "Getting lost was the best thing ever!"

Carol laughed softly, putting an arm around her granddaughter. "Sometimes the best things happen when we least expect them."

As the sun dipped low, bathing the street in golden hues, the family settled onto hay bales to watch the evening talent show. They cheered along with the crowd as locals sang songs, juggled fruit, and performed comedy skits. By the end, they felt like honorary members of the community.

When it was finally time to leave, Tom turned back onto the correct route, but none of them minded the extra miles. The detour had turned into a highlight of the trip, and the wrong turn they had taken would be remembered fondly as the happiest mistake they'd ever made.

Memory Prompts:

- Did you ever get lost on a trip?
- Do you remember stopping at roadside diners or gas stations?
- Was there a time when getting lost became a happy surprise?

Conversation Starters:

- Do you like road trips or flying better?
- If you could take a road trip anywhere, where would you go?
- Do you enjoy maps or GPS more?

The Luggage with a Secret

Margaret had always believed that packing was an art, but this time she'd clearly overdone it. Standing at the crowded platform, waiting for the train, she struggled to manage her large suitcase, stuffed to bursting. As the whistle blew in the distance, signaling the train's approach, Margaret gave one final tug on the stubborn zipper, which promptly burst open, spilling the contents across the platform.

Scarves floated gently to the ground, socks scattered wildly, and her favorite cardigan landed neatly over a nearby bench. Margaret froze, mortified, while her heart thumped loudly in her chest.

Before she could react, laughter erupted around her—not mocking laughter, but the good-natured kind that warmed the heart and eased embarrassment. An older man with a broad smile knelt down to retrieve a pair of woolen socks. A young woman carefully picked up a silk scarf, dusting it gently before handing it back with an understanding wink.

"Oh dear," Margaret chuckled nervously, cheeks flushed. "This wasn't exactly how I imagined starting my journey."

"Well," said the older man cheerfully, placing a neatly folded shirt back into her suitcase, "at least you'll have plenty of room for souvenirs!"

Margaret laughed freely then, feeling her embarrassment fade away. She joined in gathering her belongings, feeling gratitude swell in her chest for the kindness of these strangers.

As they repacked, Margaret explained how she'd always been prone to packing too much. "You never know when you might need an extra sweater," she joked, gesturing at the pile still waiting to be squeezed back inside.

A lady nearby nodded sympathetically. "I once packed an entire sewing kit for a weekend trip. Never touched it."

"Well, you never know," Margaret replied warmly. "Preparation is key."

Soon, the platform was clear again, her suitcase securely zipped—this time with extra hands lending support—and Margaret boarded the train. She sat near a window, her suitcase safely tucked away, relieved yet smiling at the memory she'd unexpectedly created.

Halfway through the journey, the older man from the platform appeared in her car. "Mind if I join you?" he asked gently.

"Please do," Margaret welcomed him, pleased to see a familiar face.

"Name's Henry," he said, settling into the seat across from her. They exchanged stories easily, laughing at travel mishaps and sharing experiences from journeys past. As the landscape sped by, Margaret realized this small misadventure had opened the door to new connections she might have otherwise missed.

When the train finally reached its destination, Margaret carefully lifted her suitcase down. It seemed heavier somehow, filled not just with clothes but with warmth, humor, and the kindness she'd encountered.

"Safe travels," Henry called out cheerfully.

Margaret smiled, waving back. She knew now the secret her luggage had carried wasn't in the clothes it held, but in the laughter and companionship that spilled out along the way.

Memory Prompts:

- Did you ever pack too much for a trip?
- Do you remember using old suitcases or trunks?
- Was there ever a funny travel mishap in your life?

Conversation Starters:

- Do you prefer traveling light or packing everything?
- What's the most unusual thing you've packed for a trip?
- Do you enjoy planning or just going with the flow?

The Seaside Postcard

Helen sat on a sunlit bench, the salty breeze gently lifting her hair as waves crashed softly in the distance. On her lap were a handful of postcards she'd picked from a charming shop along the boardwalk. She carefully chose a vibrant picture showing the sun setting over the ocean, thinking warmly of her two best friends back home, Evelyn and Rose.

As she wrote, she imagined their delighted smiles when they found her colorful greetings among their bills and magazines. "Wish you were here," she scribbled playfully, detailing her adventures exploring quaint seaside shops, eating fresh seafood, and enjoying the peaceful mornings strolling barefoot along the shore.

The afternoon passed pleasantly, and soon she had written two heartfelt cards, each lovingly tailored for her dear friends. She stood, stretching leisurely, and headed toward the nearby mailbox. Lost in thought, enjoying the warmth of the sun on her shoulders, she barely noticed as she slipped the postcards into the mailbox, unaware of the delightful mix-up about to occur.

Days later, Evelyn opened her mailbox, excitedly recognizing Helen's familiar handwriting. She eagerly began reading, then paused, puzzled and amused. The card cheerfully addressed her as Rose, describing details clearly meant for their other friend. Meanwhile, across town, Rose stood at her kitchen counter, laughing at the mix-up as she read Evelyn's card.

Rose called Evelyn right away, giggling as she said, "I never knew you loved seafood so much."

"And apparently, you adore long walks at sunrise," Evelyn replied with a playful sigh. "Who knew?"

The two friends shared a laugh over the mix-up, feeling closer to each other and to Helen despite the accidental switch. Each postcard became a humorous keepsake, tucked affectionately on fridge doors as a reminder of friendship and the spontaneous joy of mistakes.

Helen returned home a week later, completely unaware of the postcard confusion. Her friends invited her to lunch, barely containing their excitement. When Evelyn handed Helen the swapped cards, she was at first horrified, then burst into laughter.

“Oh, no! I mixed up the addresses,” Helen exclaimed, covering her face with both hands. "I thought I’d planned everything perfectly!"

Rose squeezed her friend's hand reassuringly, smiling warmly. “Actually, it was perfect. We got double the fun out of your vacation.”

Soon they were recounting their favorite parts from the accidental postcards, laughing until tears gathered in their eyes. Later, when the laughter settled and dessert arrived, Helen pulled two small boxes from her purse, handing one to each friend.

"Now these," Helen teased gently, "I definitely labeled correctly."

Inside were delicate shells collected from the same beach she'd described—each small treasure a sweet reminder of the seaside adventure they'd all shared, even from afar. Helen learned that sometimes mistakes were the very things that made life—and friendship—so beautifully memorable.

Memory Prompts:

- Did you ever send postcards during trips?
- Do you remember receiving letters or cards from far away?
- Was there a trip you loved sharing stories about?

Conversation Starters:

- Do you prefer postcards or photographs as souvenirs?
- What place would you love to send a postcard from?
- Do you enjoy keeping travel mementos?

The Stubborn Suitcase on Wheels

Charles had always considered himself an experienced traveler. He prided himself on moving efficiently through airports, slipping gracefully between rushing passengers and crowded gates. But today, Charles's trusted suitcase had other ideas.

It all started when Charles hurried into the bustling terminal. He checked his watch repeatedly, realizing he'd misjudged traffic and now had only minutes before his flight began boarding. "Plenty of time," he reassured himself, gripping the suitcase handle tightly. Yet as soon as he picked up the pace, the bag wobbled defiantly, refusing to follow smoothly behind.

He tugged firmly, but the suitcase veered wildly, bumping into a display of plush travel pillows. Charles muttered apologies, quickly setting the pillows back in place, feeling his cheeks redden slightly at the amused glances of fellow travelers.

Determined, he pressed on, urging the suitcase forward. Instead, it zigzagged unpredictably, as if deliberately trying to embarrass him. Charles fought back a chuckle, realizing the absurdity of wrestling a stubborn piece of luggage through the airport.

"Oh, come on now," he whispered to the unruly bag, now fully aware of the smiles from passengers observing his struggle.

Turning a corner sharply, Charles nearly collided with a flight attendant, who gracefully sidestepped his suitcase's unpredictable path. "Having a bit of trouble?" she asked, her eyes twinkling with laughter.

"Just giving everyone a little pre-flight entertainment," Charles replied good-naturedly, managing a sheepish smile.

His suitcase seemed determined to add more comedy to the journey, choosing that precise moment to topple onto its side. Charles paused, shaking his head in mock despair before setting it upright again. "All right," he sighed, "you win. We'll take it slow."

The spectators around him chuckled warmly, their empathy clear in their smiles. A young family watched with particular delight, their two children giggling as the suitcase performed its spontaneous dance.

"At least someone's enjoying this," Charles joked, nodding toward the laughing children.

Finally, approaching his gate, Charles gently guided his suitcase, relieved they'd reached their destination without further incidents. As he settled into his seat aboard the plane, the passenger next to him turned, smiling knowingly.

"I watched your luggage adventures," the man said cheerfully. "Made my wait at the gate much more enjoyable."

Charles laughed easily, finally relaxing. "Glad I could help. Sometimes travel's best stories come from mishaps."

As the plane soared above the clouds, Charles reflected warmly on his airport escapade. He realized how much he'd enjoyed those humorous exchanges with strangers. Perhaps the stubborn suitcase had known exactly what it was doing, nudging him to slow down and appreciate the joy hidden within unexpected moments.

From now on, Charles decided, he'd embrace every zigzagging suitcase and spontaneous detour, knowing that laughter was a priceless travel companion, no matter how unpredictable the journey.

Memory Prompts:

- Did you ever travel through a busy station or airport?
- Do you remember carrying heavy bags?
- Was there a trip where packing was a challenge?

Conversation Starters:

- Do you prefer traveling with a backpack or suitcase?
- What's your favorite type of travel bag?
- If you could travel anywhere without luggage, where would you go?

The Beach Sandcastle Contest

On a warm summer afternoon, families gathered along the sunlit beach, where golden sand stretched endlessly beside a calm, glittering sea. It was the annual sandcastle competition, a highlight for both children and adults, eagerly anticipated throughout the year.

Young Ethan stood near the shoreline, carefully examining the sand. He had spent weeks imagining his sandcastle, sketching intricate towers and moats on scraps of paper that cluttered the kitchen table. Now, faced with the sprawling beach and endless possibilities, he was ready.

Beside Ethan, his parents unpacked buckets, spades, and colorful plastic molds, chatting with neighbors who had set up their own sandy workstations nearby. Laughter and friendly teasing filled the air as children raced back and forth with buckets of water, splashing their way through shallow waves.

Ethan got to work immediately, molding the base, sculpting walls, and carefully placing shells and smooth stones around the entrance. His creation soon took shape, complete with winding stairs, arched doorways, and a small, delicate tower that soared proudly at the center. His family watched with affectionate smiles, impressed by Ethan's careful focus.

Just as he stood back proudly, admiring his masterpiece, a rogue wave crept unexpectedly higher than the others. Ethan watched, frozen, as the water surged forward, swirling around his feet and reducing the carefully built structure to a gentle mound of sand and shells.

For a moment, silence fell. Ethan's eyes widened, stunned by the sudden collapse. Then, before disappointment could settle in, his father chuckled gently, placing a comforting hand on his son's shoulder.

"I think the ocean wanted to join the contest," his father said lightly, squeezing Ethan's shoulder warmly.

Laughter spread through the group as neighbors rushed to help Ethan rebuild, offering handfuls of sand and decorative stones. Soon, the entire group was working together, parents and children alike, creating something even grander than Ethan had initially planned.

As the sun dipped toward the horizon, their new sandcastle stood proudly—a masterpiece of teamwork, creativity, and shared laughter. Families stepped back to admire their creation, cheering and taking photos to remember the joyful chaos of the afternoon.

Ethan smiled brightly, no longer thinking of the unexpected wave as a disaster. Instead, it had become a favorite memory, a funny story he knew he'd retell many times. It reminded him that the joy wasn't really about building the perfect castle but about creating something special with the people he loved most.

As families packed up their beach towels and buckets, strolling contentedly toward their cars, Ethan lingered a moment. He watched as another gentle wave lapped softly against the sandcastle walls, knowing tomorrow the beach would be smooth again, as if nothing had ever stood there. Yet he also knew the laughter, camaraderie, and warmth of this day would remain forever, carved deep within his heart.

Memory Prompts:

- Did you ever build sandcastles as a child?
- Do you remember visiting the seaside with friends or family?
- Was there a favorite beach you enjoyed?

Conversation Starters:

- Do you prefer sandy beaches or rocky coasts?
- What's your favorite seaside activity?
- Would you enjoy visiting the beach today?

The Wrong Bus Ticket

Grace had always been cautious, double-checking every detail whenever she traveled. Yet today, as she climbed aboard the bus, clutching her ticket and her small suitcase, she felt strangely relaxed. Settling comfortably into a window seat, she barely noticed the route number displayed on the sign above her head.

It wasn't until the city streets began giving way to unfamiliar countryside that Grace started to sense something was off. The bus rolled gently past fields dotted with cows, then small, picturesque houses she didn't recognize. She looked down at her ticket, her eyes widening in realization.

"Oh dear," Grace murmured softly, leaning forward in concern. "This isn't the bus I meant to take."

A woman sitting across the aisle overheard and leaned closer. "Where were you headed?" she asked kindly.

Grace smiled sheepishly. "To Brentwood—but I suspect we're nowhere near there."

The woman chuckled warmly. "No, dear, this bus goes to Ashville. Lovely town, though. Maybe it was meant to be."

Grace sighed softly, her anxiety easing at the woman's gentle tone. Soon, the bus slowed to a stop, pulling into a charming little square where market stalls lined the cobblestone streets. Brightly colored banners fluttered gently, and the air was filled with the scent of fresh bread, roasted nuts, and blooming flowers.

The woman from the bus introduced herself as Martha, inviting Grace to join her as she walked through the market. With no other choice, Grace accepted, quickly discovering the delightful surprises awaiting her in Ashville.

They wandered through stalls brimming with handmade jewelry, jars of honey, and vibrant bouquets of wildflowers. At one stand, a vendor offered Grace a taste of his freshly made apple jam, the sweetness reminding her of the farm trips from her childhood.

"You see," Martha said knowingly, noticing Grace's relaxed smile, "sometimes taking the wrong road leads exactly where we're meant to be."

Grace laughed, shaking her head in gentle disbelief. "I suppose you're right."

Throughout the afternoon, Grace found herself immersed in the warmth of Ashville's people. She chatted with locals, listened to musicians performing cheerful songs in the town square, and even tasted a pie so delicious she couldn't resist buying a second slice.

As the day began to wind down, Grace sat on a bench beside Martha, savoring the final rays of sunlight as they washed over the peaceful town.

"I never expected today to turn out like this," Grace admitted quietly. "I planned everything perfectly, yet my happiest days always seem to happen by accident." Martha nodded knowingly, patting Grace's hand gently. "Life's little detours have a way of surprising us, don't they?"

When Grace finally boarded the correct bus that evening, waving goodbye to her new friend, she realized this unexpected adventure had become one of her most treasured memories. Settling into her seat, she decided that perhaps being perfectly prepared wasn't always necessary. Sometimes, she thought with a smile, the best days were the ones she never saw coming.

Memory Prompts:

- Did you ever ride a bus to a new place?
- Do you remember a time you visited somewhere by accident?
- Was there a trip that surprised you in a good way?

Conversation Starters:

- Do you prefer exploring new towns or revisiting familiar ones?
- What's your favorite market or fair memory?
- Would you rather travel in the morning or evening?

The Train Station Piano

Maggie settled onto one of the old wooden benches at the train station, glancing at her watch. Another twenty minutes before her train would arrive. She sighed gently, preparing herself for the familiar boredom of waiting. Around her, travelers hurried by, lost in their own worlds, their faces buried in phones or newspapers.

Then, a sudden, bright note broke through the usual murmur. Maggie turned, surprised to see a young man seated at an old upright piano tucked in a corner of the waiting room. She hadn't noticed the piano before, likely because it had blended into the station's aged charm, worn and overlooked. But now, beneath the musician's hands, it seemed alive again.

The melody started softly, drawing gentle attention from the waiting crowd. Conversations faded, replaced by curious glances and then genuine smiles as the music filled the space, softening the tension of travel. Maggie felt herself relax, a peaceful warmth spreading through her chest as familiar notes drifted toward her.

An elderly woman nearby hummed quietly, recognizing the tune. Soon others joined in softly, their voices creating a spontaneous chorus. A young couple swayed gently together, sharing a quiet laugh as they moved in rhythm with the music.

Maggie felt her own foot begin to tap along unconsciously, her smile widening as she caught the eye of the elderly woman beside her. "Wonderful, isn't it?" Maggie whispered, leaning closer.

The woman nodded warmly. "I haven't heard this song in years. It brings back good memories."

Encouraged by the enthusiasm around him, the young musician played more confidently, his fingers dancing effortlessly across the keys. When the first song finished, applause filled the station. He laughed modestly, nodding his thanks before beginning another tune, this one livelier, drawing even more passengers into the joyful moment.

Children spun and twirled, giggling openly now. Business travelers set aside their phones, momentarily freed from work and stress. The music had turned strangers into friends, each smile and laugh knitting the group closer together.

Maggie soon realized she no longer cared about the wait. She was simply grateful for the unexpected gift of music, which had transformed a dull afternoon into something bright and memorable.

When the musician finally stood to leave, passengers shook his hand, offering heartfelt thanks. He waved humbly, promising to return another day. As he walked away, a gentle quiet settled once more, though now it felt full of shared happiness.

Maggie's train soon pulled into the station, but she boarded with newfound joy. She knew she'd carry the warmth of that spontaneous concert with her long after her journey ended. Settling into her seat, she understood that some of life's most beautiful experiences were those that appeared without warning—quiet reminders that even a simple moment of music could bring strangers together, making the everyday extraordinary.

Memory Prompts:

- Did you ever hear music in an unexpected place?
- Do you remember waiting for a long train or bus ride?
- Was there a time music lifted your spirits?

Conversation Starters:

- Do you enjoy live music more than recordings?
- What instrument do you like to listen to most?
- Would you enjoy hearing music in a public place today?

The Map That Led to Nowhere

Laura unfolded the worn, hand-drawn map and studied it with a puzzled expression. Beside her, her friend Emily squinted at the faded lines and scribbled instructions. They'd found it tucked inside an old book at the local library, its edges slightly torn, hinting at past adventures. Intrigued, they'd decided to see where it led.

The sun warmed their shoulders as they set out on their walk, following the map's directions eagerly. It pointed toward a narrow trail, weaving gently through patches of wildflowers and tall grass. Birds chirped cheerfully overhead, their songs brightening the journey. At first, it felt as though they were heading somewhere special.

But soon, the instructions became confusing. The map mentioned a "big rock shaped like a turtle," yet every rock they encountered looked exactly like—well, just another rock.

Laura laughed, shaking her head. "Did the person who drew this even know what a turtle looks like?"

Emily chuckled, scanning the path ahead. "Maybe turtles looked different back then."

Determined not to give up, they continued, though it felt as if they were simply walking in circles. When the map pointed toward an old wooden gate, Emily laughed aloud, throwing up her hands dramatically. "We passed this gate half an hour ago!"

Laura sighed in mock despair. "I think our mysterious map-maker was just playing games."

Just as they were about to turn back, Emily pointed toward a small, overgrown path they hadn't noticed earlier. Curious, they stepped forward, brushing aside leafy branches. Suddenly, they emerged into a secluded garden bursting with wild beauty. Flowers of every imaginable color bloomed in delightful chaos, butterflies fluttered softly, and sunlight filtered gently through trees overhead.

They exchanged amazed looks. "I think we just found what the map was leading us to," Laura whispered.

They sat down together on an old stone bench nestled beneath a flowering vine, taking in the peaceful surprise. The garden was hidden and clearly untended, but something about its wild nature felt magical.

Emily smiled warmly, breathing in deeply. "Maybe the map-maker knew exactly what they were doing after all."

Laura nodded thoughtfully, appreciating this quiet place they'd found together. She knew they'd remember this adventure forever—not just for the beautiful garden they'd stumbled upon, but for the laughter, confusion, and joyful sense of discovery along the way.

As they finally walked back home, the map safely tucked away, Laura realized the journey itself had been the true treasure. They'd set out to find something hidden, but the greatest discovery was the happiness shared in moments of uncertainty. Even if the map had initially seemed to lead nowhere, it had brought them exactly where they needed to be.

Memory Prompts:

1. Did you ever follow a map or directions that were unclear?
2. Do you remember using paper maps before GPS?
3. Did you enjoy exploring new paths as a child?

Conversation Starters:

1. Do you prefer maps or asking people for directions?
2. Would you enjoy a treasure hunt?
3. What's your favorite type of walk—forest, city, or beach?

The Suitcase Full of Balloons

The family reunion had been planned for months, and everyone was looking forward to it, especially Uncle Jack. Known for his playful personality and mischievous sense of humor, Jack often had a surprise up his sleeve. This year, he'd decided to take things to another level.

On the morning of their departure, Jack carefully packed his suitcase. But instead of neatly folded clothes, socks, or toiletries, he filled it entirely with colorful balloons. After inflating each one, he carefully tucked them inside, chuckling softly to himself as he snapped the suitcase shut. His nephew, Adam, had noticed the unusual preparations and asked curiously, "Uncle Jack, what are you doing?"

Jack simply grinned, winking conspiratorially. "You'll see, Adam. Just wait."

Upon arriving at the cozy inn where the reunion was held, the family gathered in the comfortable lobby, hugging and chatting eagerly after months apart. When Jack entered, pulling his suitcase behind him, his relatives greeted him warmly, unaware of what was about to unfold.

"Did you bring your entire wardrobe, Jack?" teased Aunt Linda, eyeing the bulging suitcase.

Jack smiled mischievously. "Actually, I've brought something better."

With theatrical flair, Jack dramatically unzipped his suitcase. Immediately, balloons sprang forth in an explosion of vibrant colors, floating into the air, bobbing gently as they filled the room. Gasps of delight and bursts of laughter filled the lobby, as adults and children alike reached up to catch the drifting balloons.

"Oh, Jack!" Linda laughed, shaking her head affectionately. "You always know how to make an entrance!"

The children giggled uncontrollably, racing around to capture the balloons. Even the adults joined the playful scramble, momentarily becoming children again themselves. Grandpa Henry gently nudged

Jack's shoulder, his eyes twinkling with amusement. "You've certainly outdone yourself this time."

Throughout the afternoon, balloons became the centerpiece of the reunion, passed playfully from person to person, inspiring games, laughter, and storytelling. Later, as the family gathered around the dinner table, stories of Jack's balloon surprise spread warmly, each relative smiling as they shared their favorite parts of the playful chaos.

After dinner, Adam sat next to Jack, grinning widely. "Now I get it," he whispered. "That was the best surprise ever!"

Jack put his arm around his nephew's shoulder, smiling warmly. "Sometimes the simplest things bring the greatest joy."

As evening settled in, the balloons continued drifting quietly around the room, becoming gentle reminders of the joyful afternoon. Eventually, the laughter faded to quiet conversations, and the family sat comfortably together, sharing memories and stories under the soft glow of lamplight.

Long after the reunion ended, everyone would remember Jack's suitcase full of balloons, not just because of the laughter it sparked, but because it reminded them of the joy of simple surprises and the warmth of being together.

Memory Prompts:

- Did you ever travel with family for a reunion?
- Do you remember a playful surprise during a trip?
- Was there ever a time you packed something unusual for fun?

Conversation Starters:

- Do you prefer surprises or knowing what's planned?
- What would you pack if you could bring anything at all?
- Do you enjoy traveling to see family or friends more?

Chapter 10: Hope & Inspiration

Hope can quietly lift our spirits even on ordinary days. It often arrives in small gestures, simple acts of kindness, or comforting words when we least expect them. This chapter is filled with gentle stories that celebrate these moments of quiet optimism and inspiration. Maybe you remember placing a lantern at a window during a storm, helping someone find their way home safely, or receiving an encouraging letter from an old friend after many years. Perhaps a simple smile from a new neighbor sparked a lasting friendship, or a lost glove pinned to a fence taught you the warmth of community care. Inspiration also appears in everyday experiences like a neighborhood talent show, where courage shines brighter than talent, or a spontaneous moment of laughter during an outdoor picnic. As you read these stories, think about times when you felt encouraged by small acts of kindness, or when someone's gentle words brightened your day. These moments remind us that hope is always within reach, often hidden in the simplest actions or quietest voices. Allow these stories to gently lift your spirits, reconnect you with comforting memories, and remind you of the kindness and warmth we can always find in those around us.

The Lantern in the Storm

Thunder rattled the windows as raindrops danced like tiny drums on the roof. Inside, the warm glow of a lamp cast gentle shadows across the living room walls. Near the window, nine-year-old Lucy watched the rain streak across the glass, her small face pressed close, eyes scanning the darkened road.

Her mother walked in carrying a steaming cup of tea. "Sweetheart, come away from the window. Your father will be home soon. The storm can't stop him."

Lucy nodded but didn't move. "I know, Mom. But I want him to see us from far away."

A flash of lightning briefly illuminated the garden outside, and Lucy's mother placed the tea on the table. Seeing her daughter's concern, she had an idea. "Would you like to help me with something special?"

Lucy turned around, curiosity brightening her eyes. "Like what?"

Her mother went to the closet, pulling out a beautifully etched glass lantern, worn with age but loved dearly. "This belonged to your grandmother. She always lit it when storms came to guide your grandpa safely home."

Lucy took the lantern carefully into her hands. It felt reassuringly solid, cool metal and glass, with a little door that opened smoothly. "Can I really put it in the window?"

"Of course," her mother smiled, striking a match and lighting the candle inside. "Sometimes the smallest light can shine the brightest."

Lucy placed the lantern on the window ledge, gently positioning it where the glow could spill into the darkness. The soft flicker danced across her hopeful face as she stared into the night, her reflection mirrored softly in the glass.

Minutes passed, stretching longer than usual. Lucy and her mother sat close on the couch, wrapped in the reassuring silence broken only by distant rumbles of thunder and the steady, comforting tap of rain. Just when Lucy began to wonder if perhaps the lantern wasn't strong enough, two headlights turned onto their road.

“It's him!” Lucy cried, leaping up.

Outside, the car slowed, pulling carefully into the driveway. Moments later, the front door opened, revealing her father, damp from the rain but smiling warmly.

“Well, look at that,” he said, pointing toward the window. “I saw that light from the road. It led me straight home.”

Lucy ran forward, hugging him tightly around the waist. “I put it there so you wouldn't get lost.”

Her father knelt down, brushing a strand of hair from her face. “That little lantern made all the difference, Lucy. It reminded me I was almost home.”

That night, as the storm faded and the world outside slowly settled into peace, Lucy lay awake listening to the last gentle patters of rain. The lantern, still glowing softly by the window, became more than just a guide for her father. It was a promise, a quiet message that home was always waiting, always warm, always ready to welcome those they loved.

Memory Prompts:

- Do you remember a time when someone waited up for you?
- Did your family have special lamps, candles, or night-lights?
- What weather sounds make you feel safe indoors?

Conversation Starters:

- Do you enjoy storms or prefer calm weather?
- If you had a special lantern, where would you hang it?
- What makes you feel safe on stormy nights?

The Letter That Arrived Late

Sunlight poured gently through the attic window as Emily climbed the creaky stairs. Dust motes floated lazily through the warm beams, and the air carried the faint smell of old books and cedar. It was a quiet afternoon, perfect for exploring boxes filled with forgotten memories.

Emily paused in front of a tall chest of drawers. Curious, she pulled open the top drawer, sifting through yellowed postcards, faded photographs, and old ticket stubs. Then her fingers brushed against something tucked away in the back—a small envelope, edges curled with age.

She drew it out carefully, turning it over. Her breath caught when she saw her name written neatly across the front in handwriting she instantly recognized. It belonged to Sarah, her childhood friend who had moved away years ago. Emily had always wondered why Sarah never wrote, why their close friendship had faded into silence. And now, in her hands, was an unopened letter.

She sank onto a small wooden stool and gently opened the envelope. As she unfolded the paper, memories flooded back: laughter ringing in the schoolyard, whispered secrets during sleepovers, and afternoons spent sharing dreams under the big oak tree in Sarah's yard.

The letter began simply:

"Dear Emily,

I miss you already! It's only been a week since we moved, but it feels much longer."

As Emily read, she felt Sarah's words reaching across the years, as fresh and heartfelt as the day they were written. Sarah described her new home, her loneliness at a new school, and how much she wished Emily could visit. At the end of the letter, Sarah had written, "Please write back soon. Friends forever, no matter how far apart."

Emily stared at the letter, feeling both joy and sadness mingle inside her. The letter had gotten lost somehow, caught between layers of memories, hidden away and forgotten. She had spent years wondering if their friendship had ever mattered to Sarah, and now she realized it had always mattered deeply.

Feeling a sudden sense of urgency, Emily went downstairs, letter in hand, and found her phone. She hesitated briefly, heart racing, then searched Sarah's name. After a few moments, she found her—living just two towns away.

She dialed the number, holding her breath as the phone rang. A gentle voice answered, older now but unmistakably familiar.

"Hello?"

Emily's voice trembled slightly. "Sarah, it's me...Emily."

There was a stunned pause, then delighted laughter burst from the other end of the phone. "Emily? Oh my goodness, is it really you?"

Emily smiled, tears warming her eyes. "I just found your letter, the one you wrote all those years ago. I never knew it existed until today."

Sarah laughed softly, her voice filled with emotion. "Better late than never, right?" They talked effortlessly, catching up on their lives, bridging the gap of lost years. By the time they ended their call, they had planned a reunion, promising to never lose touch again. That evening, Emily placed Sarah's letter in a special box on her desk, smiling warmly as she did so. It was a beautiful reminder that friendship, no matter how long silent, is never too late to revive.

Memory Prompts:

- Did you ever receive a letter that changed your day?
- Do you remember a time you reconnected with an old friend?
- Was there someone who surprised you with kind words?

Conversation Starters:

- Do you prefer writing letters or making phone calls?
- Who would you write a letter to today?
- Do you enjoy keeping old letters or cards?

The New Neighbor's Smile

From the front window, Clara watched the moving truck slowly back into the driveway next door. She had lived on Rosewood Street long enough to see neighbors come and go, each arrival bringing curiosity and a touch of nervousness. Today, though, felt different. The moving van seemed especially large, hinting at a family that might be loud, busy, or perhaps unfriendly. Clara felt a pang of anxiety. She hoped for neighbors who would become friends, but you never knew.

She glanced down at the plate of freshly baked chocolate chip cookies cooling on her counter. It was a small tradition her mother had passed down to her: "Always greet new neighbors with something sweet," she'd said. But now, Clara hesitated, worried the gesture might seem intrusive or unwelcome.

Through the window, she spotted a young woman helping a small child down from the truck's cab. The woman brushed a strand of hair from her face and glanced toward Clara's window, catching her gaze unexpectedly. Clara froze for a moment, embarrassed, until the woman smiled—a warm, genuine smile that reached her eyes and immediately eased Clara's nervousness.

Feeling a surge of courage, Clara took a deep breath, picked up the cookies, and walked across the yard toward her new neighbors. With each step, her heartbeat quickened, but that friendly smile gave her comfort.

"Hi there!" Clara called out gently, holding up the plate. "Welcome to the neighborhood. I'm Clara from next door."

The woman's face brightened even more, relief mixing with genuine happiness. "Oh, thank you! I'm Maggie, and this is my son, Jack." The little boy clung shyly behind Maggie's leg, peeking out curiously at the plate of cookies.

Clara crouched down to Jack's level. "I made these fresh this morning. Would you like one?"

Jack looked up at his mother, who nodded encouragingly. "It's okay," Maggie said gently. Jack took a cookie, nibbling cautiously at first, then breaking into a big grin. Clara felt warmth spread through her heart.

Over the next hour, Clara learned about Maggie and Jack. Maggie loved gardening, just like Clara, and Jack adored animals and picture books. Clara shared stories about the neighborhood: the best parks, the library's weekly storytime, and the bakery that made amazing pies. With each detail exchanged, the initial uncertainty between them melted away.

When the sun began to set, Maggie gently squeezed Clara's hand. "Thank you for coming over," she said softly. "Moving is always stressful, but your welcome made it feel like we truly belong."

Clara smiled, realizing how quickly friendship could bloom from a simple greeting. "You do belong," she replied sincerely. "And you've already made the street brighter."

As Clara walked home, she glanced back at her neighbors now unpacking happily. Her earlier worry felt distant. Maggie's simple smile had opened the door to connection, reminding her that kindness and friendliness were always worth sharing.

Inside her home, Clara felt an excited anticipation. She knew these neighbors would become friends, and Rosewood Street had grown a little brighter, thanks to one warm smile and a plate of cookies.

Memory Prompts:

- Do you remember welcoming a new neighbor?
- Did you ever become close friends with someone who moved nearby?
- What was the first neighborhood you lived in like?

Conversation Starters:

- Do you enjoy meeting new people?
- What makes someone a good neighbor?
- Would you prefer living in a busy town or a quiet street?

The Lost Glove

A chill hung in the air, the sky heavy and gray with the promise of snow. Tommy tugged his scarf tighter around his neck as he stepped outside, his mittened hand clutching his mother's tightly. The other hand felt oddly cold. He paused, glancing down in confusion.

"Oh no!" he exclaimed, staring sadly at his bare hand. "My glove!"

His mother knelt beside him, concern and patience warming her eyes. "Did you drop it somewhere?"

Tommy nodded, embarrassed. "Maybe near the market."

Together, they retraced their steps, scouring sidewalks and shop doorways. The bright red mitten, carefully knitted by his grandmother, was nowhere in sight. With each step, Tommy felt his hope slipping further away, replaced by disappointment and guilt.

"It's gone," he said softly, feeling tears pricking his eyes. "Grandma made it special for me."

His mother gently squeezed his hand. "Maybe someone will find it and bring it back. You never know, Tommy. People can surprise you."

That night, as snowflakes began to softly drift from the sky, Tommy stared out the window. He wondered where his little red mitten was, hoping it wasn't buried under the snow.

The next morning, the neighborhood was blanketed in sparkling white. After breakfast, Tommy bundled up again, feeling sad as he stepped outside. But as he approached the corner near the bus stop, something colorful caught his eye.

There, pinned carefully to the wooden fence, was his missing red mitten. Next to it hung a small cardboard sign with handwritten letters: "Lost glove found here. Stay warm!"

Tommy's heart jumped with delight. Someone had found his glove and thoughtfully placed it where he could see. He slipped it onto his cold hand, the warmth instantly comforting. He glanced around, wondering who had been so kind, but the street was quiet and empty, covered only in soft snow.

Later, his mother smiled warmly when she saw his mitten. "See? Kindness always finds its way home."

That afternoon, Tommy and his mother made hot chocolate, and as he sipped the sweet warmth, he thought about the stranger's act of kindness. He felt a desire to pass that kindness along.

Days later, when Tommy noticed a small knitted scarf on the sidewalk, he picked it up gently, brushing away snowflakes. He carefully draped it over the same wooden fence, securing it with clothespins. He added a sign of his own: "Lost scarf found here. Stay warm!"

Tommy smiled, imagining someone else discovering the scarf, just as he had found his glove. It was like magic, the way kindness could be shared, turning disappointment into hope.

The red mitten became more than something to keep his hands warm—it was now a symbol of community care, a small reminder that even the smallest gestures mattered. And every time Tommy wore his mittens, he felt connected to the stranger who had shown him kindness, quietly promising himself to always pass it forward.

Memory Prompts:

- Did you ever lose something and have it returned?
- Do you remember wearing mittens, scarves, or special winter gear?
- Was there a time a stranger's kindness stayed with you?

Conversation Starters:

- Do you prefer gloves or mittens in winter?
- What's your favorite way to warm up on a cold day?
- Who has shown you kindness recently?

The Village Parade of Lanterns

Twilight settled gently over Willowbrook, painting the sky in soft shades of purple and gold. Children gathered excitedly in the town square, each clutching homemade lanterns decorated with ribbons, paper stars, and tiny drawings that glowed softly in the fading daylight.

Maya held her lantern carefully, its paper sides painted with delicate butterflies. Her eyes shone with pride; she'd spent the entire afternoon carefully crafting it with her grandmother. Beside her stood her friends Lily and Ben, their lanterns glowing warmly, casting cheerful circles of light around their feet.

“Is everyone ready?” called Mrs. Thompson, the schoolteacher whose voice was as gentle as a lullaby. Children nodded eagerly, their faces reflecting both excitement and wonder.

Slowly, the parade began to move, lanterns lighting up the winding streets of the village. As they walked, neighbors stepped onto porches or leaned out windows, waving and smiling. The soft murmur of conversation filled the air, punctuated by bursts of laughter as lanterns bobbed gently in the evening breeze.

Maya glanced around, soaking in the warmth of the moment. It was magical, the way the lanterns danced like fireflies, illuminating the familiar streets she loved. She felt safe and happy, comforted by the presence of friends, family, and neighbors.

At the corner by the bakery, Mr. Hanson waved from his porch, holding a tray filled with freshly baked cookies. “Stop by after your walk!” he called, grinning warmly. “Hot chocolate for everyone!”

The children cheered, their lanterns bobbing more energetically now. As they continued their journey, the gentle sound of footsteps echoed softly against the cobblestones, blending beautifully with the quiet laughter.

Near the end of their route, Maya noticed an elderly woman standing by herself on the sidewalk. The woman's expression softened as the parade approached, her eyes twinkling as she admired the children's creations.

Maya hesitated, then stepped toward the woman, lifting her lantern higher. "Would you like to join us?" she asked softly.

Surprise blossomed into a radiant smile. "I would love that," the woman replied, reaching out a gentle hand.

Together, they walked the last stretch of the parade route, Maya's lantern casting a warm glow between them. By the time they reached Mr. Hanson's bakery, Maya had learned that her new friend's name was Rose, and that she had grown up in Willowbrook, attending the same lantern parade when she was a little girl.

Rose's stories fascinated Maya, filling her with a sense of connection to something bigger than herself. The parade, she realized, wasn't just about the lanterns; it was about the people who carried them, the memories they shared, and the joy of walking together.

Later, as everyone gathered around tables set up outside the bakery, Maya sipped her hot chocolate, feeling warmth both inside and out. The street was alive with friendship and laughter, the lanterns glowing softly, creating a scene that felt timeless and perfect. As the evening drew to a close, Maya walked home with her grandmother, lantern swinging gently by her side. She smiled, already imagining next year's parade, eager for another chance to share the simple magic of light and community.

Memory Prompts:

- Did you ever carry a lantern or candle in a parade?
- Do you remember nighttime walks with family or friends?
- Was there a festival in your town you looked forward to?

Conversation Starters:

- Do you prefer daytime or nighttime celebrations?
- What colors remind you of joy?
- If you made a lantern, what design would you choose?

The New Shoes at Church

Sunlight spilled through the stained-glass windows, filling the small church with vivid patches of color. Tommy sat proudly beside his mother, legs swinging gently from the polished wooden pew. His new shoes gleamed brightly—shiny black leather, perfectly smooth, with laces tied into neat little bows. He couldn't stop staring at them.

"Sit still, Tommy," whispered his mother with a gentle smile, placing her hand lightly on his knee. He nodded, doing his best to remain calm, but excitement bubbled inside him. These were special shoes, his first pair that didn't pinch or squeeze his toes.

When the service began, the congregation rose together. Tommy stood, feeling very grown-up. As he shifted his weight, his shoe made a sudden and unexpected squeak. The sound was sharp and clear, echoing through the silence of the church. Tommy froze, cheeks flushing bright red.

His eyes darted nervously around the congregation, certain everyone was staring. But instead of stern looks, he saw gentle smiles and eyes twinkling with warmth.

As the pastor continued speaking, Tommy tried again to stand very still. But his shoes seemed determined to cause mischief, squeaking loudly with every tiny movement he made. Soon, he heard muffled giggles spreading through the congregation.

Tommy's embarrassment deepened. He stared down at his shoes, wishing he could melt into the floor. Suddenly, the pastor paused and looked directly at Tommy with a kindly smile. "It seems someone's shoes have decided to join the sermon today," he said, eyes sparkling with gentle humor.

The church erupted into friendly laughter. Tommy's mother squeezed his shoulder reassuringly. Tommy looked up at her, surprised to see her smiling warmly. "It's all right, sweetheart," she whispered. "We've all had squeaky shoes at least once."

Tommy relaxed a bit, realizing no one was upset. In fact, the congregation seemed delighted by the unexpected interruption. Mr. Johnson, who sat in the pew behind them, leaned forward and whispered with a smile, "I had shoes just like those when I was your age. Squeaked louder than yours!"

As the service continued, Tommy's shoes occasionally chimed in, drawing smiles and gentle laughter each time. By the end, Tommy found himself smiling too, realizing the squeaks weren't something to worry about after all.

After church, several members of the congregation approached Tommy, sharing memories of their own funny mishaps as children. Tommy listened eagerly, comforted and amused. His shiny new shoes, he realized, had made him feel closer to everyone around him.

On the walk home, Tommy skipped lightly, shoes squeaking merrily along the sidewalk. His mother laughed softly. "You seem happier now."

Tommy nodded, grinning widely. "I thought everyone would be upset with me, but they were kind."

His mother took his hand gently. "We all have moments like that, Tommy. It's good to laugh, especially at ourselves."

Tommy smiled, looking down again at his shoes. Their squeaks had taught him something important: sometimes, the very things that make us feel awkward can bring us closer to those around us. And, squeaky or not, he decided his shoes were perfect just the way they were.

Memory Prompts:

- Did you wear special clothes to church or gatherings?
- Do you remember getting new shoes or a new outfit as a child?
- Did you ever feel shy about standing out?

Conversation Starters:

- Do you prefer shoes that are stylish or comfortable?
- What was your favorite place to visit as a child?
- How do you like to celebrate special days now?

The Traveling Hatbox

Martha settled into her seat on the train, arranging her belongings neatly around her. The familiar click and sway of the carriage gently reassured her, a pleasant reminder that she was on her way to see her sister, Ellen, after months apart. At her feet sat a round hatbox, faded but elegant, holding her favorite blue hat decorated with a silk ribbon. It had been a gift from Ellen, and Martha never traveled without it.

As the train picked up speed, Martha leaned back and closed her eyes, lulled by the rhythmic motion. Suddenly, she felt something brush past her ankle. Startled, she opened her eyes to see the hatbox gently rolling down the aisle toward the front of the carriage.

"Oh, dear!" Martha exclaimed, quickly rising from her seat and moving after it. But each time she got close, the gentle sway of the train nudged the hatbox just out of reach.

Passengers began to notice, smiling at the comical chase. A young girl giggled softly as Martha tried again and missed. An elderly man reading his newspaper chuckled quietly to himself, folding the paper and setting it aside. "Looks like you've got a runaway," he teased warmly, rising to help.

"I suppose I do," Martha laughed, cheeks rosy from embarrassment but smiling despite herself.

Soon, others joined in the playful chase. A woman wearing bright glasses set down her knitting needles and tried to catch it, only to have the box spin away mischievously. A little boy eagerly reached out, nearly grasping it before it gently rolled onward, drawing amused laughter from everyone watching.

Finally, the hatbox bumped softly into the conductor's polished shoes at the far end of the carriage. With a wide grin, he lifted it up triumphantly, holding it above his head as if it were a great treasure. "Does this little traveler belong to someone?"

Martha stepped forward, blushing but smiling broadly. “That would be mine. Thank you.”

Returning to her seat, she carefully placed the hatbox next to her, securing it firmly this time. Passengers around her shared amused glances, breaking into easy conversation. The young girl asked Martha about her destination, and the elderly man recounted a similar incident from his own travels long ago.

Martha felt warmth spreading through her. Her mischievous hatbox had transformed strangers into friendly companions. She soon found herself swapping stories and sharing laughter, forgetting how long the journey was or worrying about losing her hat again.

When the train reached her station, Martha stood, hatbox safely in hand, smiling warmly at her new friends. The elderly man tipped his cap, saying kindly, “Safe travels—and hold tight to that hat!”

As Martha stepped off the train onto the bustling platform, she spotted Ellen waiting, waving eagerly. Ellen's eyes immediately fell upon the hatbox, and she laughed knowingly. “Did it behave this time?”

Martha chuckled, shaking her head. “It caused quite the scene, actually, but I wouldn’t trade it for the world.”

Together, arm in arm, they walked away from the station, the hatbox securely under Martha's arm—a cherished companion whose playful escape had brightened her day and forged new connections.

Memory Prompts:

- Did you ever carry something unusual on a trip?
- Do you remember a time when luggage caused a funny problem?
- Was there a favorite hat or item you took everywhere?

Conversation Starters:

- Do you like planning trips or being spontaneous?
- What was your most memorable travel companion?
- Would you rather visit a new city or return to a familiar place?

The Picnic Blanket Escape

It was one of those sunny spring afternoons when everything felt fresh and full of promise. The Henderson family arrived at Riverview Park, their baskets overflowing with sandwiches, sliced fruit, and lemonade. The grassy field was dotted with families enjoying the warmth, and laughter drifted through the air.

Sara and her brother, Liam, carefully unfolded the large red-and-white checked picnic blanket. Together, they stretched it flat across the soft grass, placing heavy baskets on each corner to anchor it down.

"Perfect!" their mother said, setting out plates and cups neatly, arranging food and treats in an inviting spread.

But just as everyone began to settle down, a gentle breeze whispered through the trees. Then, without warning, a sudden gust lifted one corner of the blanket, sending napkins fluttering and plastic cups rolling away.

"Oh no!" cried Sara, lunging forward to catch the blanket. Liam tried to help, but before they knew it, the wind swept under the blanket like a playful spirit, lifting it clear off the ground.

"Quick! Catch it!" laughed their father, jumping to his feet as the blanket soared just out of reach. It billowed like a sail, teasingly floating higher and farther away.

Soon, the whole family was chasing the runaway blanket across the park. Sara sprinted ahead, giggling breathlessly as the cloth danced through the air just beyond her fingertips. Liam stumbled after, laughing too hard to keep up. Their mother called out instructions between bursts of laughter, but the mischievous blanket simply spun and twirled, delighting in its newfound freedom. Nearby, other families watched, smiling and pointing at the joyful scene unfolding before them. A group of children playing tag paused their game, joining in the chase with shrieks of delight.

"Almost!" shouted Sara, stretching out her arms. But the blanket swooped upward again, drifting gracefully toward a nearby duck pond. Everyone gasped, certain the picnic blanket would land in the water. But instead, it settled softly onto a nearby bush, draping itself neatly over the branches.

The crowd cheered, clapping and laughing as Sara and Liam triumphantly reclaimed their runaway treasure. The children carefully lifted it from the bush, shaking out a few stray leaves and twigs, still giggling uncontrollably.

When they returned to their spot, their father secured the blanket firmly to the ground, anchoring every corner with extra care. Families who had watched the spectacle waved cheerfully, some even coming by to joke about the adventurous picnic blanket.

As they finally sat down to enjoy their meal, cheeks flushed and eyes sparkling with happiness, Liam sighed dramatically. “Who knew picnic blankets could be so sneaky?”

Their mother smiled, pouring lemonade into cups once more. “It turned out to be a lot more exciting than our usual picnics, didn’t it?”

Sara nodded, nibbling her sandwich, eyes bright with excitement. “Maybe next time we should bring ropes.”

The laughter that followed carried gently across the park, blending perfectly with the sounds of birdsong and distant play. Even though the picnic had started with unexpected chaos, it became a day filled with warmth, friendship, and a memory that would bring smiles long after they packed up their baskets and headed home.

Memory Prompts:

- Did you ever try to keep a blanket or rug from blowing away?
- Do you remember outdoor games with family?
- Was there a time you laughed at a funny accident?

Conversation Starters:

- Do you prefer quiet days outside or busy ones?
- What’s your favorite kind of outdoor food?
- Have you ever had a day that turned out better because of an accident?

The Town Talent Show

It was a warm Friday evening, and the little community hall was buzzing with excitement. The townspeople had been preparing all month, and now, the annual talent show had finally arrived. Chairs were lined up neatly, and strings of cheerful lights sparkled softly above the wooden stage.

Emma sat in the front row, clutching the edge of her seat, her heart pounding with a mix of anticipation and nerves. She had practiced her song countless times, singing quietly to her stuffed animals and bravely in front of the mirror, but tonight was different. Tonight, everyone would be watching.

Beside her, Grandpa Jim squeezed her hand gently. "You'll be great, Emma. Just have fun," he whispered, smiling warmly.

The show began with Mr. Peterson, the baker, who attempted juggling muffins with great enthusiasm, sending pastries tumbling to the floor. The audience laughed kindly, applauding his cheerful effort. Next came Mrs. Thompson, the librarian, whose magic tricks left everyone puzzled, especially when she accidentally revealed where she had hidden the rabbit. But laughter and encouragement filled the hall, reassuring every performer.

Emma watched her neighbors step bravely onto the stage, each bringing laughter and applause, no matter how their act turned out. When Mrs. Mayfield sang off-key, the audience sang along gently, their voices blending in kindness and camaraderie.

Finally, Emma's name was called. Her breath caught, but she felt Grandpa Jim's comforting squeeze once more. With shaky legs but determination in her heart, she climbed the stage steps, the bright lights softening as she stood before the microphone.

At first, Emma's voice came out softer than she intended, barely audible. She hesitated, eyes wide with fear, until she spotted Grandpa Jim smiling encouragingly from the front row, his eyes twinkling with pride.

Taking a deep breath, Emma sang again, her voice clearer and stronger. The audience listened, smiling warmly as her confidence grew with each note. By the final chorus, everyone was clapping along, their joyful faces lifting her spirit higher than she'd ever imagined.

As she finished her song, applause erupted from every corner of the room. Emma beamed, cheeks flushed with happiness. She felt proud—not only because she had sung well, but because she'd been brave enough to try.

After the performances, everyone gathered for refreshments and laughter. Emma hugged Grandpa Jim tightly. "You were right, Grandpa," she said, eyes sparkling. "It really was fun."

He smiled gently, patting her shoulder. "You showed courage up there. That's the greatest talent of all."

Later that evening, families and friends chatted happily beneath the warm glow of lights, sharing stories of their favorite moments from the show. Emma felt deeply connected to everyone, knowing each performer had stepped forward bravely, just like her.

The talent show wasn't about perfection. Instead, it celebrated courage, joy, and the laughter shared among neighbors. Emma knew she would always remember this night as the moment when she learned that sometimes, the simplest acts of bravery could bring the biggest smiles.

Memory Prompts:

- Did you ever perform in front of a group?
- Do you remember attending a school or town show?
- Did anyone in your family love to perform?

Conversation Starters:

- Would you rather sing, dance, or tell a story on stage?
- What kind of show do you enjoy watching?
- Do you like being in the spotlight or cheering from the audience?

The Festival of Lights

It was early evening in Maplewood, and already, tiny golden lights twinkled gently in every window along Main Street. Excited voices filled the air as families stepped outside, each holding carefully crafted lanterns in colors of amber, violet, and sky blue. Tonight was the town's annual Festival of Lights, a tradition everyone eagerly anticipated.

In her family's small garden, Sophie adjusted the delicate paper lantern she had carefully decorated with stars and moons. Her parents watched warmly, holding lanterns of their own, softly glowing against the twilight.

"Are you ready, sweetheart?" her father asked gently.

"Yes!" Sophie replied, eyes shining. Tonight, she had a special wish to make.

The streets soon filled with neighbors, each person hanging their lanterns on tree branches along the sidewalks. The gentle glow grew brighter, creating a magical pathway that seemed to stretch toward the stars. Sophie felt warmth spreading inside her as she walked beside her parents, listening to neighbors greet one another with laughter and cheerful conversation.

They passed Mr. and Mrs. Hartley, who waved enthusiastically from their porch, lanterns sparkling above their heads. Further along, Sophie saw her best friend, Ava, holding a lantern covered in shimmering butterflies. The girls exchanged excited waves and big smiles.

As night deepened, the trees became filled with lanterns of every shape and color, gently swaying like softly glowing leaves. The town transformed into a wonderland of light, guiding them toward the old oak in the center of Maplewood, where everyone gathered to share wishes and dreams for the coming year.

When Sophie reached the oak, she lifted her lantern and carefully hung it on a low branch, watching its soft glow mingle with the others. Around her, families shared their wishes aloud. Some wished for health, others for happiness, some simply for more days filled with moments like these.

Sophie closed her eyes briefly, took a deep breath, and spoke clearly: "I wish that we always have nights like this, with everyone together."

A quiet warmth settled over the gathering, and neighbors smiled gently at each other, murmuring softly in agreement. Sophie's mother hugged her, eyes bright with affection. "That's a beautiful wish," she whispered.

As the evening continued, laughter echoed softly through the streets, mingling with the gentle rustle of lanterns swaying in the breeze. Children chased fireflies beneath the trees, their delighted shouts filling the air, while adults shared memories and friendly conversations beneath the warm glow.

Eventually, families began drifting back home, lanterns still glowing warmly in the darkness, leaving the town bathed in comforting light. Sophie walked home slowly, holding her parents' hands tightly. She glanced back one final time at the glowing trees, committing the beauty and warmth of the evening to memory.

In bed that night, Sophie listened to the gentle wind rustling softly outside her window. She felt happy and hopeful, reassured by the memory of lanterns lighting the way home, each one a promise of another year filled with warmth, kindness, and joy.

Memory Prompts:

- Did your family have traditions with lights or candles?
- Do you remember festivals or fairs at night?
- Was there a tradition that made you feel hopeful?

Conversation Starters:

- Do you prefer candlelight or bright lights?
- What's your favorite season to celebrate?
- What tradition would you like to share with others?

A Final Note

Dear Reader,

Thank you for spending your valuable time with these stories. I hope they brought you smiles, comfort, and moments of reflection. Every story shared within these pages is intended to spark conversation, inspire memories, and remind us of life's simple joys.

Your honest opinion matters deeply, not only to me but also to fellow readers looking for meaningful stories that speak to their hearts. By taking a brief moment to leave your genuine review on Amazon, you'll help others discover this book and perhaps rekindle their own treasured memories.

Whether your feedback is positive, negative, or somewhere in between, please know I genuinely value your perspective. I will personally read every single review.

Thank you again for sharing your thoughts, and for being part of this journey.

Warm regards,

Ted.

Scan to leave a review on Amazon

www.ingramcontent.com/pod-product-compliance
Lightning Source LLC
Chambersburg PA
CBHW081134300726
48982CB00005B/968
9781806472376